Bandits on the Rim

Bandits on the Rim

G. Kent

Copyright © Gary R. Kent
April 2012
All rights reserved.

ISBN-10: 0615613667
ISBN-13: 978-0615613666
LCCN: 2012937736

To The Best Mountain Slippers:
Larson, Dunham, and J.

A Tenacity Press Book

Tenacity Press, founded by Hal Zina Bennett and Susan J. Sparrow in 1992, follows the tenets of a literary cooperative. We join an honored tradition of small publishers who, through the centuries, have championed the works of fine authors. For more information:
www.TenacityPressbooks.org

CONTENTS

PART ONE

1.	Hughes Supermarket	1
2.	Slippery Air	6
3.	Chili Beans	12
4.	Crossing to the Other Field	15
5.	The Doggy Bowl	21
6.	Maray Point	25
7.	Dr. Kildare	27
8.	Burgundy Wine	33
9.	The Cop Who Shot Himself	36
10.	The Bracelet	40
11.	An Elderly Man	44
12.	The Widow Ms. D.	47
13.	Mountain Slipping	53
14.	Freedom	55
15.	Yosemite	61
16.	Monopoly	70
17.	Halloween 1974	79
18.	Green Glass	87

PART TWO

19. Lillian's Music Store	92
20. Mt. Pinos	97
21. The Hiking Boots	102
22. The Morning After	105
23. Lake Buena Vista	109
24. Morphine	118
25. Butterscotch Creek	121
26. Mission de San Fernando	124
27. Fire of '47	126
28. A Very Fine List	133
29. Red Flag	134
30. Harry Kay's Letter	138
31. Tunnels	141
32. First Win	143
33. The Grassy Circle	146
34. No More Beliefs Forever	151
35. That Evening	153
36. Decoy	155
37. The Orange Porch Light (Is On)	158
38. Organ Pipe	161
39. The Orange Porch Light (Is Off)	164
40. Harry Kay	166
41. Mr. Cuddy	169
42. Queen of Hearts	174
43. Blue Mountain	176
44. Return to Hughes Supermarket	188

PART ONE

ONE
Hughes Supermarket

A typical November morning in the Valley

The widow Ms. D. continued to exhort Woody. She never realized the black Lab was dead.

On this wickedly delicious morning at Balboa and Devonshire, as the sky dripped with luminous clouds and blue honey, the widow Ms. D. jerked her black Seville from the path of an empty shopping cart that was rolling across the parking lot, and drove through a plate window at Hughes Supermarket. Her lower lip ceased to quiver—end of doggy dialogue—but her big toe throttled the gas pedal and punched the Seville into a *TV Guide* and gum rack at cash register number 9.

Fortunately, the crabby cashier had wandered off to confirm the price of New and Improved Tums, or she would have been missing in action. This Seville was taking no prisoners.

"That rich lady's black car is out of control," Larson had commented a moment earlier. He was holding a *TV Guide* open to the evening schedule.

"No." J. insisted. "It's only a teenager fucking around."

"That's no teenager," I said, "nor is she fucking around."

"Fucking around or not," Dunham said, "that Seville has definitely hopped the tracks."

I glanced at Larson's *TV Guide*. "Hey, Dun. Check out Elvira." Channel 9's campy Fright Night seductress grinned from the page. "What a mink."

"Mistress of the Breasts," Dunham agreed.

Larson perked up. "What about breasts?"

"Fright Night is on TV tonight."

"What's the flick?"

"*The Return of Count Yorga.*"

"Too avant-garde."

"Beware of Robert Quarry."

"Please," J. said. "John Carradine is the vampire extraordinaire."

I shook my head. "Doesn't touch Christopher Lee in *The Horror of Dracula.*"

"No actor can snarl like Jack Palance."

Larson said, "How can you compare those amateurs to Bela Lugosi?"

"Bela Lugosi?" Dunham laughed. "He's so queer."

"Lugosi is the original spook."

"I liked *The Fearless Vampire Killers* with Roman Polanski."

"Right, Dun."

"Hey, Dun," I said, "did Julie Christie play the female lead in *Vampire Killers*?"

"No, it was Sharon somebody."

J. thought for a moment. "Never heard of her."

Larson pulled me aside. "Remember the day of my accident in Organ Pipe?"

"Sure."

"Remember we spoke of a Mexican bandit?"

"Joaquin Murrieta."

"Right, Murrieta."

"What about him?"

"I think I just saw him in the Hughes Supermarket parking lot fucking with your 340 Duster."

I said, "Larson, Joaquin Murrieta was killed over a hundred years ago by Captain Harry S. Love."

"Yeah, well, Joaquin is pointing to the black Seville too."

L.A.'s Balboa and Devonshire trembled. Shards of Hughes plate window rained into the supermarket, whistling over my head and shattering on the counters and floor.

Snatching my leather coat for support, J. slung me into the *TV Guide* and gum rack and took the brunt of the incoming missiles. Juicy Fruit and Doublemint gum littered the floor. A sheet of glass smashed onto the counter and exploded, nipping his ear and throat.

"Jesus, Kay," J. said. "Count Yorga bit me." As he sank to the floor, his middle finger ripped the buttons off my leather coat.

Ms. D.'s Seville clubbed Dunham in the hip and lifted him into the air. Sliding over the waxed hood, he bounced off the windshield, shooting cracks into the glass.

"Kay," he hollered. His body catapulted into a shelf of chili beans. I shrugged helplessly, still gripping onto our chocolate bars.

"Hey, lady," I shouted, forming a finger cross, "there's a new invention. It's called brakes." With an accelerated surge, Ms. D.'s Seville rumbled down the length of aisle 9, the nose of its hood nudging me along like I was wearing roller skates, and finally crashed into a freezer door. My butt was rudely introduced to ice cream.

Blood rushed out my nose, though I wasn't certain whether it was mine or J.'s.

Spitting on the hood of the car, I wiped my nose with a sleeve. The smell of vanilla slipped under the blood.

Suddenly, all by itself, a shopping cart zoomed down aisle 9 and bashed into the rear of the Seville. Its added impact seemed to crush me. A wave of nausea leaped up my throat.

"Hey, Kay."

"Larson, my butt's eating ice cream."

The blow from the shopping cart also bumped Ms. D.'s head into the automatic gearshift, slipping it into neutral. When her big toe jacked the pedal, the engine roared furiously against my ribs. I glared at her through the shattered windshield.

"Not enough mayhem, Widow D.?" I snapped, baring my teeth. "Maybe for an encore you can pancake the Mexican bandit fucking with my 340 Duster."

Next to Ms. D. in a disheveled heap was Woody, the dead black dog. I wondered how the Lab had died.

Larson said, "Hey, Kay, how do you know she's a widow?"

Larson had escaped with no wounds. He appeared by my side, ghostly and translucent, resembling Bela Lugosi in the classic vampire film *Dracula*.

Yanking Ms. D. by the hair, Larson dragged her body, clumsy in death, out of the driver's seat. When she plopped next to the front tire, I felt a pang of guilt for haranguing a stiff.

As the Seville lurched into reverse, I tumbled onto the slopping ice cream cartons and slid into

Ms. D. I was in too much pain to slither away. Instead I touched her arm, but it was already cold and hard like the surface of a storefront mannequin.

Larson rolled me onto my back and squatted down just in front of my face. He said, "Quit faking, Kay. You're not dead."

"Remember the two Indian girls in the blue pickup outside of Gila Bend?"

He leaned closer. "Shiny black hair at eighty miles per hour."

"Wish we would've tried talking to them."

"Stick around, Kay," he said in a sobering tone.

Opening one eye, I said, "No Elvira tonight."

TWO
Slippery Air

*After the accident, Kay follows
Larson to Blue Mountain.*

Sixty miles north, Blue Mountain's crater summit bulged from a caramel haze blanketing Cuddy Valley. Lining its sharp ridges, clusters of Jeffrey pine resembled an army of Mexican bandits.

Swooping into the timber, I dared not glance back at Balboa and Devonshire. In the rubble of Hughes Supermarket was a shopping cart and black Seville, quarts of blood mixed with vanilla ice cream, chili beans, chocolate bars, Ms. D., and morning chardonnay breath.

Snow hadn't stuck in the Tehachapi's, but the wind was raw and crisp. A cross breeze, smelling of butterscotch, swooshed up a pant leg, tingling my testicles.

Larson moaned. "Jesus, right up my pant leg."

"Cheap thrill."

"Right, Kay, most refreshing."

Tossing Larson a pair of Red Rooster work gloves, I pulled mine over my knuckles with my teeth. "Never saw weather like this up here," I said. "Temperature on the porch post was nine degrees."

Following a path behind my cabin, I weaved between the scrub and piñon pine. At the end of the trail, a slope leaped sharply for nearly a thousand feet to Maray Point on the tip of Iris Ridge. Outlandish territory. At the edge of Maray Point stood a preposterous great southern oak with a full canopy of Spanish moss.

Gulping water, I spilled it over my chin. "Hey, Larson, my nose won't stop bleeding.

"You drink water like it's chardonnay."

"Dunham said the same thing."

"Dunham can be eerie."

I said, "No, he's harmless."

"If you say so."

From Maray Point we trudged up Iris Ridge to Butterscotch Creek and the legendary 27 giant Jeffreys. They could be clearly spotted from Frazier Mountain Highway, towering four times higher than any other tree in the Los Padres National Forest.

Lounging on the 28th tree, that had crashed over Butterscotch Creek and formed a bridge, Larson uncorked a bottle of chardonnay while I dug into my pack and retrieved our crab sandwiches from the Rustic Grill in Granada Hills.

We snacked in silence.

Suddenly a red-tailed hawk appeared, banking above Maray Point and zipping below the tree line.

I said, "Watch, Larson, red-tails love to nest in that creepy oak." When there was no answer, I turned to look. He had taken the bottle of chardonnay and departed.

"All summer I've dreaded going back to Organ Pipe." Larson had admitted at Maray Point. "But it's not only my accident that intrigues me. Joaquin Murrieta is waiting."

"Dunham's tagging along."

"Keep him on a leash, Kay."

"He's harmless," I insisted.

"He's my friend too, but no one who dreams about the future is harmless."

"He'll be on his best behavior."

"I'm not afraid of another accident, Kay, or of dying. No one has failed at dying. I assume I'll be successful too."

I said, "Why do you talk that way? You had a decent fright. Your number slipped to the bottom of the chart."

"It may come up today on Blue Mountain."

"Mine too. So what? Wouldn't be bad going out with a buddy."

"Not too bad."

"No more drudgery at work."

"You're a wiseass, Kay."

"Your accident is still fucking with you."

"But I'm not afraid of dying anymore," he insisted. "Sierra del Ajo took me by the throat and slapped me off its ledge. But I was lucky. My friends hauled my ass back to the 340 Duster." He patted my shoulder.

"Let's take my 340 Duster to the desert."

"Of course."

"Don't die more than once, Larson."

"It's my indulgence."

"Don't feel like the Lone Ranger."

"In dreams I steer myself back to that morning on Sierra del Ajo and relive the accident, hoping to discover a clue that will lessen my fear. Some nights I wake in utter horror and I'm compelled to run laps around my coffee table. Other times I sit in the bathtub and concentrate on the girls I've fucked, until I become erect and cheerful. If I can manage an erection I can't be dying."

"I'll store a mental note."

"Remember the movie *Deliverance*?"

I nodded.

"In Organ Pipe I battled with the intensity of Burt Reynolds and Jon Voight, but felt like Ned Beatty sloshing in the mud and helpless, while getting fucked in the butt. Joaquin is waiting for me."

"Maybe Joaquin fancies your 'purty mouth'."

"You're a wiseass, Kay," he repeated. "But you know I touched 'it' in Organ Pipe."

"I know."

Lightning pricked Blue Mountain's crater summit. Shielding my eyes from the flash, I peeked through my Red Rooster work gloves and saw an image of the bolt fading softly. Its thunder rumbled between my teeth, however, and gave my heart a solid punch.

On the shore of Butterscotch Creek, Larson set up a perimeter between two white firs. It began to hail bits of glass but I was protected by the 27 big trees, towering four times higher than any other tree in the Los Padres National Forest. Larson received a minor pummeling. As the storm quickened its pace, he spotted my position and saluted with his fist.

One year ago, on Arizona's Sierra del Ajo, Larson, J., and I had chalked our hands and scaled a seventy-foot wall to a barren ridge. Ten feet from our destination, Larson quit climbing and dug his heels into a small ledge so he could relax and savor the rugged Organ Pipe. "Go up without me," he said. "I want to listen to the Sonora." When J. and I hesitated, he cried, "Jesus, we're not musketeers, you know. How did John Muir ditch his mo-ron buddies?"

"Okay, okay," I said. "Big man." J. and I finished the climb.

From the ridge, a grove of saguaro cactus on the desert floor resembled the bandits on Blue Mountain. In a few moments, J. sauntered to the edge to check on Larson. Suddenly he stumbled back and placed a hand over his mouth. I sprinted to the edge and looked down. Larson had plunged sixty feet and lay sprawled on the rocks.

"How could it happen?" I blurted. "There was no sound."

"Nothing I'd want to hear," J. said.

"John Fucking Larson Muir."

By the time J. and I had muscled him off Sierra del Ajo and across the Sonora, I thought he was a stiff. In the backseat of my battered 340 Duster, he resembled Bela Lugosi at the conclusion of the classic vampire film *Dracula.*

Earlier, around the campfire, we had joked about one of us slipping off Sierra del Ajo. Instead of hysterics, we had joked that the survivors would be pissed about having to lug back a carcass.

Now the sky was hurling baseballs. Unsheltered from the ferocity of the hail, Larson was barely visible.

"Did you see him, Kay?"

I glanced around. "No."

"He's here too."

"Who?"

"Murrieta."

"Larson," I shouted, "Larson, come here." But Larson wouldn't budge. Instead he blended into the hail and disappeared. His tactic intrigued me.

Scrambling off my log, I raced along Butterscotch Creek and searched the ice for his tracks.

Not a trace.

"Kay," Larson yelled. "Stick around, Kay." His voice had the same sobering tone as it did in Hughes Supermarket on Balboa and Devonshire in Granada Hills. Sneaky bastard had backtracked and was lounging on the fallen 28th log. During our game, the brutal hail had changed to a gentle snow.

THREE
Chili Beans

Kay learns how to bark.

"Hey, Kay," Larson said, "medic has arrived."

"Is all this shit mine?" I asked, incredulous, surveying my blood-sodden shirt and Levi's.

"J. has a claim to a pint or two."

"Quick, Larson, check my dick."

"You're doing fine, Kay."

"Why is the medic taking my pulse?"

"Medic shit."

"Hey, buddy," I said, "if I'm still talking I must be pulsating."

"Shut up, Kay."

I said, "Now he's poking my ribs. Please, Henry, not the ribs."

Larson said, "It's okay, Garrett. He's a medic."

"Actually, I'm a veterinarian," said the medic. He nodded to me. "My office is on Devonshire right next door to the supermarket."

"Garrett lives in Sepulveda."

"Well, when Garrett recovers he can bring his pooch or Felix by for a free stool check."

I said, "Not the ribs, Henry."

"Why do you call me Henry?"

"You even talk like Henry."

"Who?"

"Doc," Larson said, "Kay's right. You look exactly like Dr. Henry Kissinger."

"No shit?"

I said, "Larson, did Henry Kissinger ever date Julie Christie?"

"Not to my recollection."

The vet said, "Let me hear you shout, Garrett. When a patient is in shock, a good shout can relieve the pressure."

"What?"

"I tell all my patients to bark if they're distressed."

"You want me to bark?"

Larson said, "Go ahead and bark, Kay. It'll make you feel better."

"Henry's not a medic," I said, "he's a dog vet."

"It's what he claims."

"How's J.?"

"I hear him cursing, naturally. It'd take an ICBM to shut up J."

"How's Dunham?"

"Keep breathing, Kay."

"What about Dunham?"

"I don't know. Fuck."

"What's wrong?"

"Dunham disappeared."

"What do you mean, disappeared?"

"The Seville must have knocked him through the roof."

With two fingers, I motioned him to come closer. "This is no reason to indulge."

"I need to sit in my bathtub."

"Don't die more than once, Larson," I repeated.

"Why was I spared?"

"Who better?"

"Don't say that, Kay."

"Then be useful. Buy some chardonnay."

13

"What for?"

"Could be my last bottle for a while."

"But where's Dunham?"

I lifted my head. "He's under the chili beans."

Larson snapped to attention. He wanted to locate Dunham, but hadn't the slightest idea which way to go. Then he looked on the back wall and found the food directory. Chili Beans—Aisle 11.

FOUR
Crossing to the Other Field

*The exchange of drugs is the
second oldest profession.*

The kitchen door had a slow creak. Dunham said, "Did you get it?"

"Yeah, did you?"

"Yeah."

"Fantastic. Let's eat first."

Normally it was my passion to fix a proper meal, delicious with a touch of artistry, and the preparation similar to foreplay. Blessed by too many Henry Miller novels, I suppose. Tonight, however, there was only confusion and gloom. With my bloodied nose pressed against the east window of my writing room, I tried to imagine Harry Kay hoofing along Iris Ridge on Blue Mountain.

"Never put a good chardonnay in the freezer, Kay," Dunham said. "It messes up the chilling process."

"It's only Gallo."

"You'd drink it right off the shelf, wouldn't you?"

"If required."

"You feeling okay?"

"Not really."

Somehow I had convinced myself of the dismal notion that Harry Kay had died, but couldn't recall any details. There had been no phone call or letter. Actually there was only a crumpled note taped to the refrigerator in strange handwriting.

"Grandfather H. Kay—Expired," it read.

"Do you have many regrets, Dun?"

"Some." He looked over the cabin. "This place is spooky, Kay. Why did you move up here?"

"It seemed like a good place to make a stand."

"Hmm, that clears it up."

"Larson just told me to bark."

"It might make you feel better."

"I'm feeling pretty worthless."

"Harry Kay wouldn't agree."

I said, "What do you know about Harry Kay?"

"I saw him hoofing along Iris Ridge."

"Is Harry Kay a stiff?"

"Read your note."

"What's wrong with me, Dun? My grandfather dies and I don't even attend his funeral."

"How could you possibly go to Harry Kay's funeral? Don't you remember?"

"I forgot. I've been sick."

He opened the refrigerator. "You're no different than anyone else. It happens to me too."

"What happens?"

"You think your feelings are unique, but that's a laugh. No such thing."

"Hmm, that clears it up."

"Ready to bark?"

"Maybe later."

"Then point me to the wine glasses, your Gallo should be imperfectly chilled."

"You're a rare buddy, Dun."

"You smeared nose blood on the window."

I said, "Let's drink chardonnay."

Dunham had brought three pounds of Alaskan king crab and stuffed potatoes from the Rustic Grill in Granada Hills. It was my job to provide salad, olives, bread, four bottles of chardonnay, and chocolate bars from Hampton's Village Market in Lake of the Woods.

Dunham said, "It's obvious why you're so jumpy, Kay. You've been mixing it up with Larson."

"So?"

"Since his accident, Larson has become eerie."

"He says the same about you."

"What do you say?"

"I tell him you're harmless, but I'm not certain."

"Larson's too caught up in his desert mystic crap. It's waiting for us too."

"What's waiting?"

"Sierra del Ajo, and a sneaky Mexican bandit."

"How do you know? You haven't been to Organ Pipe."

"Don't you remember? I had a bloody good dream about Organ Pipe."

"When?"

"On Half Dome in Yosemite."

I nodded with respect. "Keep it mum, pal." At times his dreams were uncanny. Last year he had warned Larson about his fall on Sierra del Ajo. Well, not exactly. He said J. and Garrett would have to carry Larson's ass back to my 340 Duster. He claimed to have dreamed about that too. No one took him seriously. We had joked that Larson would merely be on another tequila binge.

I said, "Do you believe in Joaquin Murrieta?"

"The Mexican bandit?"

"Hero to some."

"Well, in my dream…"

"Ixnay on the Half Dome, Dun. I don't want to know what's going to happen until it happens."

Dunham smiled. "I don't know what's going to happen."

I nodded. "Then keep your mouth shut."

"Not a word. But I wouldn't indulge myself over Sierra del Ajo."

"How do I not indulge?"

"By accepting whatever happens and moving on."

After dinner I brought out my razorblade, petrified rock from Organ Pipe National Monument, and worn fifty-dollar bill, while Dunham poured a large glass of milk. In the center of the living room we hunkered next to the potbelly stove and spread our wares on my Navajo rug.

Once or twice a season we traded cocaine for codeine and got high together. Dunham ingested my codeine while I snorted his cocaine. We both drank chardonnay.

While I cut my cocaine and chopped it into two thick lines on the petrified rock, Dunham washed down four codeine pills with the milk.

Dunham said, "Want me to save two codeine pills? Help you crash later."

"Who wants to crash?"

"Codeine is a fantastic dreamer."

I said, "Fucks up my stomach. But let's make a deal. I'll drop two codeine if you snort two lines."

"No way. I'll stick to the ceiling."

"I'll drink to that."

"Don't hog the chardonnay."

I said, "Let's go into the field. Bring the last bottle."

"Where are the chocolate bars?"

"In my pocket."

It was normal conditions on the back porch. Orange porch light shone on the mist and the temperature on the porch post was—polish the glass—forty-seven degrees. Behind my cabin was a rumpled field, bordered by piñón pine and choked with shoulder-high grass.

Wading to the middle of the field, I balanced on a concrete marker where an old Labrador had been buried. WOODY, read the marker. How the big black dog had died was a mystery.

It was soothing to stand on the grave.

On the east side of the field, Dunham pointed to a small light blinking in the piñón pine. He wanted to investigate.

"Wait, it's someone with a flashlight."

He said, "No, it's a reflection of something. Look, it's fading with the sunset."

"Let's shoot a flare."

"Saddle up, Kay."

Trailing with extreme reluctance, I scanned the trees and brush for enemy movement. In the darkness, our chocolate bars slipped from my pocket. Suddenly, we stumbled into another field, identical to the original. Instinctively, I steered to the spot where Woody was buried, but there was no concrete marker in the new field.

"Kay," Dunham yelled. "Hey, G. Kay." He was standing among the border pines waving our chocolate bars. "Let's go in the cabin and watch TV."

"What?"

"*Night Gallery* with Rod Serling."

FIVE
The Doggy Bowl

*Slipping into shock is not unlike
slipping into a warm bath.*

"Henry," I said, "where were you when the Seville hopped the tracks?"

"Pet food aisle."

"Lucky."

"She made a stupendous blast. Did the Seville push you all the way down aisle nine to this freezer door?"

"It felt like I was wearing roller skates."

He said, "You'll recover, Garrett. I've seen Chihuahuas in much worse condition and in a few weeks they're chasing the same garbage truck."

I started to speak, then choked on my spittle.

"Don't talk," the dog vet said. "No need to talk or move. Ambulance is almost in the parking lot."

There was a conspicuous pressure on my chest, as if someone were leaning on me with his foot. I asked, "What the fuck is this?" A blue doggy bowl sat on my heart.

The dog vet said, "It's a gift from the pet food aisle. If you feel sick, barf into the doggy bowl."

Not unthinkable. "How did you know I might barf?"

"Actually I brought it for your buddy. He looks pale and sickly. It's funny, in my profession the animals are the patients, yet it's the owners who barf."

"Why?"

"Owners can't handle the sight of their pet's blood."

I tilted my head. "If Larson is going to barf, why is the doggy bowl on my chest?"

He said, "No, Larson is okay. After you slipped into shock, you had a dry heave."

"Barf into the doggy bowl, Kay," Larson said. "You'll feel better." He was planted beside my left leg.

"I'm slipping, Larson. Did you feel like that on Sierra del Ajo?"

"Easy, Kay. You're not dying. Soon you can forget about this place."

"What are you doing?"

"Squeezing your leg."

"Is it bleeding?"

He said, "A dab."

"I can't breathe. It feels like a rib punctured my lung."

"Don't talk, Kay."

"I'm scared. I need to think about the girls I've fucked."

"Want me to name a few?"

"Not yet."

"Don't bring it to Hughes Supermarket."

"Bring what?"

"Sierra del Ajo."

"John Fucking Larson Muir." As my fingers clutched the doggy bowl, the lights in Hughes Supermarket began to change colors like the sky over Blue Mountain.

"At ease, soldier," the vet barked. My chills instantly retreated. "Spread your arms on the floor and stare at the ceiling. Concentrate on expanding your lungs. Inhale, exhale. Repeat it. Inhale, exhale."

"Inhale, exhale."

Staring at the ceiling, I noticed the Food Directory and located pet food—aisle 4.

Larson's grip on my left leg was beginning to smart. When he pushed the hair out of his eyes, I saw his hand was sticky with blood.

He said, "It's lousy combat, Kay. Think about the girls you've fucked."

"Have you checked my dick yet?"

The vet wrestled with an improvised tourniquet. "You're quitting. Don't give the Seville the satisfaction."

My senses seemed to heighten. An ambulance siren wailed on Balboa. At checkout stand number 9, the crabby cashier was blabbing about her incredible good fortune while fiddling with a pack of New and Improved Tums.

"Never put a tourniquet on a victim unless you're a qualified professional," the ambulance man said. "He could lose a leg if you screw up."

"I am a qualified professional," said the dog vet. "I'm a vet."

"I don't give a flying fuck if you were in Vietnam."

Larson eyeballed the man coldly. Pointing at me, he said, "He's my friend. I'm not going to watch him bleed to death. Besides, you dopey bastard, this guy's a veterinarian, not a marine."

"Yeah, well, your buddy is going to be okay. Don't worry about him. Let's go,
get him up."

"Wait," the dog vet said. "You forgot his bowl." The blue doggy bowl was placed back on my heart. When he stood up, I noticed he was wearing a long gray overcoat.

I said, "Thanks, Henry. You're a fine medic."

SIX
Maray Point

Kay nearly dies in the ambulance.

On the CBS Late Show, Marilyn Monroe was slumming with cowboys and card sharks in an Arizona saloon. "Good Lord," I said. "Look, Dunham, what a mink." In the next film, Humphrey Bogart cuffed little bug-eyed Peter Lorre and we both had a hearty laugh.

At last I struggled to sit up and cut another line of cocaine. Glancing into the petrified rock from Organ Pipe National Monument, I noticed Larson and Henry the dog vet peering over my shoulder. In the reflection, my face appeared cold and hard like the surface of a storefront mannequin.

My eye widened and the petrified rock slipped from my hand. For an instant, I thought I had been staring at Ms. D. in Hughes Supermarket.

Dunham had dive bombed at 3 a.m. Snatching my Red Rooster work gloves and leather coat, I dashed onto the wooden porch and basked under the orange porch light. My brooding over Harry Kay had receded. Perhaps I was mistaken. Blue Mountain was playing tricks. Harry Kay was probably ice fishing on Lake Vermillion in northern Minnesota.

I punched into the woods. A pound of snow fell from a piñón pine and plopped on my head. "Nice," I said, "pick on the little guy."

At the tip of Maray Point, Blue Mountain's breath licked my eyes with wet snow. Temperature on the porch post was forty-seven degrees. It seemed much colder. Flopping on my back, I watched the stars glitter on the ceiling of Hughes Supermarket on Balboa and Devonshire.

"I'll phone Harry Kay in the morning," I decided, "if I can locate my telephone."

Except for my hands and face, I was smothered in snow. Its blanket felt warm and toasty. My hands took on the pallor of a stiff. It was my chosen place and time. I had accepted Blue Mountain as the spot where my life should end, and settled on the precise moment too.

"He's losing too much blood," the ambulance man said. "Apply more pressure, and don't let him fall asleep again."

Using my hiking boots as skis, I steered toward Maray Point. The wall beneath Iris Ridge was nearly vertical. Whacking the great southern oak with my left hand, I leaped into Blue Mountain's wet breath. On impact, the mushy snow was slippery and quick.

With inexplicable determination, I galloped down the path to my cabin, covering the thousand yards in less than three minutes. It appeared I was training with the intensity of my senior cross-country season. Granada Hills had been L.A city champs in 1964.

The owl-shade lamp still glowed on the Navajo rug. Codeine dreams swarmed in Dunham's head. It seemed sacrilegious to return to my warm and cushy existence after nearly dying on Maray Point.

Stomping my boots under the orange porch light, I noticed the temperature had dropped to nine degrees.

SEVEN
Dr. Kildare

Medical procedures often suck.

"If you don't urinate I'll insert a tube."
"What?"
"Listen up, marine."
"Nothing I want to hear."
"If required, the bladder can be emptied with a tube."

Blue Mountain had faded, replaced by a brick basement reeking of sweat and medicine. "Purple Haze" by Jimi Hendrix blared on the radio. Henry the dog vet had been replaced by a real doctor who was busy gouging his fingers into my bladder. It seemed I held an ocean of urine.

I said, "Can't piss."

He handed me a large plastic bottle. "Okay, listen up (he checked my name tag), Kay. Here's the game plan. Stick Little Kay in the bottle and open fire." I grunted with true grit but there wasn't a drop. It became apparent we weren't alone. Twenty or so young people, dressed for the beach, stood around the basement taking notes.

I said, "Time out."

"What's wrong?"

"I can't piss with those teenagers staring at me."

"Jesus, this happened all the time in 'Nam. A guy would get shot and he couldn't piss for a week."

"Are you a vet?" I remembered the ambulance man didn't give a flying fuck if the dog vet had been to Vietnam.

"Army medic, 1965."

"I'm sorry, but I can't piss."

"If you don't urinate, I'll insert a tube."

"Why?"

"You must urinate before surgery."

"Who are you?"

"My name is Dr. Kildare."

"Dr. Kildare?"

"Yeah, just like the TV show."

"Please don't use a tube."

"Hey," Dr. Kildare yelled at the students from College of the Canyons. "Shut off the fucking radio and turn on a water faucet. I want him to urinate in the bottle."

Tap water gurgled softly. "Relax," he said. "Imagine yourself filled with beer."

"Can't piss."

"Imagine the joy of pissing into Olympia's famous artesian Tumwater."

"What?"

He said, "It's a joke. In 'Nam, everyone wore a T-shirt with a guy pissing into Olympia's Tumwater. Caption read, 'It's the Water.'"

"I drink Olympia."

"C'mon, buddy, relax. You're okay. You are not dying."

"I'm slipping. Did the guys in 'Nam feel that way?"

"Ambulance man claimed he 'died' for a moment on the ride over from Hughes

Supermarket," a student from College of the Canyons whispered.

"Messy internal hemorrhaging," said another.

I said, "Maybe I'll urinate on your leg."

"What?"

"It's a joke," I said. "George C. Scott pissed on Jack Palance's leg in *Oklahoma Crude*."

"I remember. Good flick. Who was the blonde?"

"Bonnie Parker."

"Great eyes, but that's not her name."

"She's a mink, but not my little favorite."

A red-haired nurse with pouty lips peeked over Dr. Kildare's shoulder. "They're ready for him in X-ray," she said.

"Take him," Dr. Kildare said. "Persuade him to piss in the bottle."

"Will he really insert a tube if I can't piss?"

"It's Dr. Kildare's decision."

"Gruesome."

"Try to relax."

I said, "Normally I love to piss. I'd love to take a piss with George C. Scott."

"What's wrong?"

"Accident must have scared the piss up me. Dr. Kildare said it happened in Vietnam. It may be a chili bean stuck up my dick." She giggled. "That's it, I got a chili bean from Hughes Supermarket stuck up my dick."

She said, "You'll push it out. At least you still have a sense of humor."

"When a doctor speaks of inserting a tube, you can either laugh or puke with equal enthusiasm."

"A bit of the Valley wit, I see."

"You look exactly like the movie star Julie Christie," I said. "Julie Christie is a mink, especially in *McCabe and Mrs. Miller*."

"Is that a movie?"

"What's the matter," I said in my best Warren Beatty voice, "you got a turd in your pocket?"

Julie Christie giggled.

There was an impressive row of wrinkles on the x-ray man's forehead. It seemed obvious he cared about his people. When he tried to flip me on my belly, I fought him like a gator.

"Goddamn it, has anyone given him a needle yet?"

"Nope."

"Give him two. I can't do shit."

At last, a man with a plan. Demanding a needle made the x-ray man my new best friend. He still appeared down in the dumps so I decided to cheer him up.

"You okay?"

"I see good soldiers fucked up every day."

I said, "Know what? Dr. Kildare's going to insert a tube if I don't piss." Instead of a smile, the x-ray man grimaced. "But who can piss with a chili bean stuck up his dick?" That softened him. "Man, I can't piss. I've got a chili bean from Hughes Supermarket stuck up my dick." Despite enormous effort, the x-ray man laughed out loud.

"All mangled up and he's still a wiseass."

Julie Christie zipped into the X-ray room with a hypodermic in her hand. Pinching the skin on my hip, she poked the needle into the fold and squirted hot morphine. Suddenly my balls and butt were drunk.

Julie Christie said, "He needs to urinate before surgery."

"Dope will relax his bladder."

Instead, a wave of nausea roller coasted up my rib cage. Anticipating the vomit, I clutched onto the doggy bowl and struggled to lift my chin. The x-ray man rushed to my side and held my head. I decided to cheer him up again. As we waited out my sickness, I made up a little joke. I said, "Am I high or is this how it feels to die?"

As Julie Christie leaned forward to wipe my face with a wet cloth, I sniffed her neck and felt the warmth of her breasts. "Am I high or is this how it feels to die," I repeated, winking at her left tit.

In spite of himself, the x-ray man burst out laughing. "All mangled up and he's still a wiseass."

Julie Christie wheeled me into a narrow corridor with a low ceiling. She said, "We're going to put you in room nine with a Los Angeles policeman. He suffered a terrible accident this morning. He shot himself while putting his pants on."

"What? I'm sorry." I had wandered into another room to watch the A.M. Movie on KTTV. Paul Newman was womanizing and kicking Texas ass.

"You're going to share a room with an L.A. policeman who shot himself."

"This morning?"

"You guys will get along famously. He's hilarious."

Oh, boy, I thought, a funny cop who does six-shooter tricks. Two hospital aides snatched control of my stretcher. Lingering in the corridor, Julie Christie was the spitting image of Mrs. Miller.

"That dopey cop was lucky," one of the aides whispered to the other. "He could have done some real damage, if you get my drift."

I said, "He could have shot off his whanger."

"What?" He tapped the other aide. "He's got big ears."

"Hey," the other aide said. "How'd you get all mangled?"

"A car fucked me up."

"What kind of car?"

"A Seville with a big whanger."

They eyeballed me suspiciously.

"All mangled up and he's still a wiseass," one said to the other. The other nodded.

EIGHT
Burgundy Wine

Jesus drank barrels of wine.

Whisked into room 9, I slipped into the air and found a warm spot on the TV. *The Three Stooges* was on KHJ.

With fiendish efficiency, a platoon of attendants tumbled into the room and began introducing my body to Mr. Equipment. Grim looking needles sucked or injected, while the enema smelled ghastly. Surging up the wall to the TV, warm water flooded my eye sockets.

From my perch on the TV, I cringed at each procedure, but the body on the bed was quiet and listless. It had long ago surrendered.

"Dr. Howard, Dr. Fine, Dr. Howard."

Posting guard with my medical chart, Dr. Kildare attracted my attention by waving a catheter. From the warm spot on the TV, I channeled all my mental energy to shoving his face into the enema pan.

"He's convulsing, Dr. Kildare."

"Wedge the doggy bowl under his chin."

It was extraordinary. My body was mangled, but in the slippery air there was no sensation other than the warmth from the TV. My awareness heightened. On the other side of the room I felt the presence of the cop who shot himself. He was watching intently.

33

Dr. Kildare said, "Let it come, Kay."

"No problem."

"Barf into the doggy bowl."

At last I was able to inspect the damage. My trunk was spotted with bright purple contusions, especially near the kidneys. I had an Appaloosa butt too. RN's discussed a punctured lung and gobs of internal bleeding. Just below the knee was a shocking Frankenstein gash. When soapy water slipped into the wound and licked a nerve, my body electrified.

"Dr. Howard, Dr. Fine, Dr. Howard."

"Still no urine," Julie Christie said.

"Give him more dope. That will relax his bladder."

I said, "X-ray man said the same thing."

"Let's do surgery."

As they wheeled me down the narrow low-ceilinged corridor, I followed the procession at a safe distance. There was an intense pressure below my belly button. Lifting my head, I tapped Julie Christie on the shoulder. "May I have the plastic bottle?"

My entourage cheered. With the entire procession stalled in a crowded lobby, Dr. Kildare winked at me and put the little glass tube in his pocket.

"Glad that ordeal is over," he said. "Jesus, I nearly stumbled into your enema pan."

Popping Little Kay into the bottle's mouth, I blasted a thick stream of Burgundy wine into the clear plastic.

When the parade continued to surgery, I decided to return to the TV and the cop who shot

34

himself in room 9. On KNXT the Lone Ranger and Tonto were riding gangbusters.

NINE
The Cop Who Shot Himself

*Sometimes there is a cop around
when you need one.*

"Hey, Sleeping Beauty," the cop who shot himself said. "Don't pretend your roommate's a stiff. I caught you eyeballing me."

Real funny dude. When the cop who shot himself winked at me and grinned, I continued to ignore him.

He tried again. "Hey, John Muir. I'm talking to you, Loco Loco."

"Whaa-at?"

"Tell me about the desert."

"What desert?"

"Sierra del Asshole or something. You played hide and go seek among the cactus."

"What?"

He said, "Jesus, a broken record. You played a game with Larson and a Mexican bandit."

I lifted my head. "How do you know about Sierra del Ajo?"

"You were blabbing in your sleep."

"What else did I say?"

"You said the game was scary."

"What game?"

The cop appeared exasperated. "The hide and go seek nonsense in the desert,
Loco Loco."

From the hallway, the jingling of a tray of blood samples caused the cop's face to blanch. For a moment, he held his breath. When no one entered our room, the cop slowly exhaled.

I said, "Did you really shoot yourself?"

"Flesh wound."

"Julie Christie said it was 'terrible'."

The cop scratched his head. "Who is Julie Christie?"

"Red-haired nurse with the pouty lips."

"Where's Sierra del Asshole?"

"Organ Pipe National Monument in Arizona. And it's Sierra del Ajo."

"When did you get back home?"

I said, "Still on my way. Only made it to Hughes Supermarket on Balboa and Devonshire."

"My apartment is on Balboa and Devonshire."

I tilted my head. "I'll store a mental note."

He said, "You're kind of a wiseass, aren't you? Where do you live?"

"San Franciscan Apartments on Nordoff. Well, I used to live there. My new home is a cabin in Lake of the Woods near Blue Mountain."

"Isn't that mountain near Lake of the Woods called…"

"Yeah, but locals call it Blue."

"Don't fuck with me."

"I'm not fucking with you."

"I don't like people who fuck with me."

"I'm not fucking with you," I repeated.

"Did you see the car when it hit the Hughes Supermarket window? Kildare said you landed butt-first into a freezer door. In the ER you were still sloppy with vanilla ice cream."

"Slid down the aisle like I was wearing roller skates."

"You kept your balance down the entire aisle?"

"It was aisle nine."

"So?"

"This is rooooooom nine."

"You're fucking with me again. I can't believe you're still alive."

"Why?"

"C'mon, Loco Loco. Even you must admit you're fucked up to the max."

"Why do you call me Loco Loco?"

He said, "If you think you're okay, you're crazy times two." Just then an elderly nurse waddled into the room with a tray of jingling blood samples. The cop who shot himself threw a blanket over his head. The nurse sloshed the alcohol and poked my arm with a fat needle.

I said, "Hey, hero, it's my turn." As blood spurted into the hypodermic, I couldn't help but observe the cop's blanket was trembling. Staring at the ceiling, I pretended not to notice. When we were alone again, he kicked the blanket off his head.

"It's a game I play with the old battleship."

"If you say so."

"I'm going to put the blanket back on my head."

"Wait, what else did I say in my sleep?"

He said, "Answer my question first. How did you like the desert?"

"It was our annual rock climbing trip to southern Arizona. Temperature was in the 50's during the day; nights were stone cold. No rain. At sunset, we built bonfires and yipped with the coyotes."

"Pleasant trip?"

"Quite. What else did I say?"
"You said you enjoyed the game."

TEN
The Bracelet

*It's best not to check the
color of your urine.*

On the TV screen, my battered 340 Duster fishtailed over Tejon Pass and careened into the back lot of Hampton's Village Market in Lake of the Woods, scattering a column of shopping carts. My face punched the steering wheel.
"Damn it."
J. said, "Slick parking, Kay."
"Didn't notice the curb."
"Your nose is bleeding."
"It's been doing that lately."
"The scratch on my neck still drips too."
Blue Mountain towered over the town of Lake of the Woods. Its crater summit made it appear like a dormant volcano. J. and I hoped to reach the summit before sunset.
I said, "I know a shortcut to the summit."
"What shortcut?"
"Butterscotch Creek. Think we can beat the sunset?"
"That would require a killer pace, Kay."
"Don't forget my shortcut."
Glancing at the shadow creeping up Iris Ridge, J. said, "Let's make a wager."
"Wager?"
"Let's bet we're sipping chardonnay on the summit of Blue Mountain before
sunset."

"Sun already has a pretty decent head start."

"Don't back down, Kay."

"I'm not backing down. What are we going to bet?"

"You don't understand," J. said. "It's a bet with ourselves. We say we can beat the sunset and the world thinks otherwise."

"Perhaps Blue Mountain would like to bet."

"Isn't that mountain called…"

"Locals call it Blue."

"Then it's settled. Blue Mountain will score the bet."

"What's our wager?"

J. said, "Only thing I have of value is my next moment."

"Let's hope your next moment includes buying a bottle of chardonnay."

"You're a wiseass, Kay. Let's bet our next moment we can whip the sunset."

"Keep it under control, J."

"That's how you bastards talk about me, isn't it?"

"Yeah, I suppose. If we win?"

"Any wager is possible."

I said, "Led Zeppelin in my living room."

The shadow crept up Iris Ridge to Maray Point.

"Awesome, Kay."

In the backcountry above Iris Ridge, J. and I got lost in the timber. Young Jeffreys grew in such close proximity that the lower dead branches created a formidable obstacle. Using my Red Rooster work gloves, I punched our way through the woods and left a trail littered with kindling.

Under the legendary 27 giant Jeffreys, I took a drink at Butterscotch Creek. No breaks, however.

At the edge of the remote burnt-out area, we stopped to piss. Yellow steam rose from my urine. After I finished, the steam hung in the air and changed colors. Its final wisp was burgundy.

J. said, "We lost time in the timber."

"Did you see my piss?"

"My urine has blood too."

Only the burnt-out area separated us from the crater summit of Blue Mountain. After nearly thirty years, the burnt-out area still reeked of incinerated pine.

At the tree line, J. popped the cork on the chardonnay and produced two wine cups from his coat pocket. Just as we stepped under the crater, the sun dipped behind Mt. Pinos in a flash of green.

"Shit."

J. said, "Nipped at the tape." His laughter tumbled into the shadows of Cuddy Valley. "We owe Blue Mountain."

Refilling my cup with chardonnay, I glanced across Cuddy Valley at Mt. Pinos. Oddly, both mountains are the identical height—9001 feet—but share no other feature. Blue Mountain crackles with energy while Mt. Pinos is an unkempt cemetery.

There was a muffled voice from Mt. Pinos, haunting and familiar. "Kay. Hey, G. Kay." Slipping across Cuddy Valley, it erupted into a piercing howl. I cupped my ears.

For a moment, time had stopped. My world was shattered. Ice cream and broken glass covered my chest. Staring at the reddened ceiling behind Mt. Pinos, I thought of nothing but the moment.

In the dirt, I noticed a faint sparkle. Half buried on Blue Mountain was a delicate silver bracelet with a Spanish design. I looked at J., but he was squatting on the rim and not taking the slightest notice of anything.

With little effort the tiny bracelet shook free from the moist dirt. It was slightly blemished, like Blue Mountain. A small burnt smudge marred the silver.

"Sounded like a wolf," J. said, "or Larson."

I nodded.

ELEVEN
An Elderly Man

Fresh needle marks usually mean good times.

On the other side of room 9, the cop who shot himself was shuddering and clutching his stomach. He was in obvious distress. My finger tapped the buzzer.

"Yes?" said the nurse.

"What's wrong with the temperature?"

"It's quite pleasant at the front desk."

"It's the North Pole in room nine."

"Who is this? The cop or wiseass?"

"Wiseass, I guess."

"Please don't play games with me."

I said, "There's something wrong with the cop who shot himself."

"Dr. Kildare just finished his rounds."

"Send him back."

She said, "He won't authorize another shot of morphine, Wiseass."

"Right, nurse."

Clicking on the light, I glanced at my new silver bracelet from Blue Mountain. Then I saw the fresh needle mark.

"Lights out room nine," a grumpier nurse barked over the intercom.

"Nurse Ratched," I muttered.

In the dark, I detected an elderly man lying in the cop's bed grinning at me. This disturbing image forced me to sit up and take notice. I clicked the light back on. The cop who shot himself was propped up in bed with his arms folded.

"What are you doing, Loco Loco?"

I was speechless. "Are you okay?"

"Me? Are YOU okay?"

I said, "It was a nightmare."

"What?"

"I must have had a nightmare."

"But you were fooling with the lights."

"Yeah, I got worried."

"Why?"

"I thought you were having a seizure or something," I said. "The temperature was vicious cold."

"Feels okay now."

"When I first turned off the light, I swear I glimpsed an elderly man in a long gray overcoat lying in your bed."

"Who do you see now?"

"You."

"Loco Loco."

I bit my lip. "It was a nightmare. You seemed distressed."

"Why would I be distressed?"

"Forget it, dude. I didn't mean to annoy you."

The cop smiled. "Don't be cross, Kay. You didn't annoy me. I'm touched you were concerned."

"Lights out room nine," the grumpy nurse repeated.

"Using my bedpan, ma'am."

I said, "Don't provoke this one. She hides our piss bottles."

"Hey, Kay," the cop said. "Why did you turn on the light?"

"What?"

"You turned on the light a second time because you saw an elderly man lying in my bed. Why did you turn on the light the first time?"

"My bracelet was hurting me."

"Your hospital bracelet?"

"No, my silver bracelet from Blue Mountain," I said, holding up the arm with the needle tracks.

For a moment, he eyeballed me suspiciously. Then he burst out laughing. His silly cackling was so infectious I started to laugh too. We howled until a nurse came over the intercom and threatened us with enemas.

I said, "Hey, nurse. Who controls the thermostat? Dr. Howard, Dr. Fine, Dr. Howard?"

She said, "All mangled up and he's still a wiseass."

"I get it," the cop said, between fits of laughter. "I fuck with you so you fuck with me. Nurse is right, you are a wiseass."

"I am aware."

"Hey, did you see Dr. Kildare?"

I said, "Sure, Dr. Kildare was here too."

The cop who shot himself visibly stiffened. "For you or me?"

"Me, I think. What do you mean, you? You're in no danger."

"Fucking A."

TWELVE
The Widow Ms. D.

*Don't shoot the messenger,
even if he is fucking with you.*

"Hey, hero," I said. "If you're going to tell the story, take the blanket off your head."

"Is the old battleship gone?"

"With my blood, not yours."

"Okay, no blanket."

"And for the moment, no drugs."

"It's odd that my errant gunplay and your accident in Hughes Supermarket happened at the same time. In my situation, someone else was involved."

"You weren't alone?"

"Allow me to reveal an important piece of the puzzle. In my building lives an old widow whose apartment is directly below mine. Every time she uses the elevator to go to her second floor apartment, she forgets to press the number two button and the elevator automatically takes her up to the third floor. Since the widow thinks she's on the second floor, and her apartment is directly below mine, she always heads straight to my door and jiggles the lock with her key. Usually she realizes her mistake and returns to the elevator. Other times I'm forced to open the door and shoo her away. She can be a real nuisance.

"Normally, I'm prepared for the widow's shenanigans. In fact, on the morning in question, I saw her pass my kitchen window and anticipated the jiggle. Then, while I was putting my pants on, I noticed the safety on my new issue nine-millimeter had slipped, and lost track of the widow. Suddenly, there was a loud knock on the front door. The widow has never knocked, she has only jiggled the lock."

I said, "Hold it, this is sounding like an accident."

"Weird, ain't it?"

"But you said it only appeared to be an accident."

"Just fucking with you."

"What about all this cash you keep mentioning?"

"Do you want to hear the story or not?"

"Yeah, sure."

"It was more than a flesh wound."

"How much more?"

He said, "The widow's knock startled me, forcing my hand to flinch. The nine-millimeter blasted my lower thigh. Bullet shattered the bone, causing splinters to poke through my skin. It was such a rude awakening I momentarily lost my voice. My only hope was to catch the widow before she made it back to the elevator. Ironically, for being so small, she drives this huge black Seville. It would have made a cool ambulance."

"Did you say black Seville?"

"But when I reached my door, the hallway was empty except for a rusty shopping cart from Hughes Supermarket."

"How did you get help?"

"Major dilemma. Sprawled on the carpet, with a finger plugging each hole, I dialed the emergency number with my fucking nose. Endured fifteen minutes of sloshing in my puke and urine. Then, all the way to Valley Hospital, the medics kept yapping about a horrific accident at Hughes Supermarket."

"Not too horrific."

"In the emergency room, Dr. Kildare said my bullet passed through the floor and struck the head of a widow's pet Labrador in a downstairs apartment. Now I really feel like a shit. I fucked up some poor dog."

I was flabbergasted. "Where do you live?"

"Corner of Balboa and Devonshire."

"In Granada Hills."

"Across from Hughes Supermarket."

I looked into his eyes. "Don't fuck with me."

"I'm not fucking with you."

"Someone told you more about my accident and now you're fucking with me."

He shook his head. "It's the truth."

"Why didn't you tell me this sooner?"

"By the way, is there a Larry in your family?"

"Harry."

"That's right, Harry Kay."

"What about Harry Kay?"

"I can't tell you."

"What do you mean you can't tell me?"

"Kildare will tell you."

"Tell me what?"

"I can't say."

I said, "You can tell me about sloshing in your puke and urine, but not about my grandfather?"

He sighed. "Okay, okay. Kildare said your grandfather, Harry Kay, died in northern Michigan."

"Minnesota."

"You were in a stupor when he came with the news. He left this note." Grandfather H. Kay—Expired, it read.

"I don't understand."

"Your grandfather is a stiff, Kay. Sorry, but you forced me."

"Why would Dr. Kildare tell me he's dead? I already know Harry Kay is dead."

"How could you know? Kildare said he died this morning. You said yourself you haven't been home."

"Harry Kay didn't die this morning. He died before I went to Organ Pipe."

"Kildare said he died this morning."

"Ridiculous. There was a note on my refrigerator in Lake of the Woods." I looked at Kildare's note again.

"Kildare also told me you live on Nordoff and Sepulveda."

"What?"

"C'mon, Kay. You're on morphine."

"So?"

"You dreamed about your refrigerator."

"No."

He said, "Kay, you think tomorrow is today and yesterday tomorrow."

"I know when Harry Kay died," I roared. "He was my fucking grandfather."

"Fucking okay."

At that moment two doctors marched into the room to inspect the cop who shot himself. They were strangers to me. One doctor poked his finger into the cop's belly.

"Does this hurt?"

"No."

"This?"

"Not really."

The doctor nodded and both left the room. But in the hallway they lingered near the door and conferred.

The cop who shot himself whispered, "What are they saying?"

"Can't hear them."

"Listen."

"What's the big deal? He didn't even look at your leg."

"Shut up. Just listen."

"Still can't hear them."

"Shit."

I said, "I'm sorry I shouted at you. I've been grouchy about Harry Kay."

"No problem."

"Why did he press your stomach?"

"I don't know. He does it every evening."

"Why don't you ask what he's doing?"

"You kidding? He's a doctor. He won't tell me."

He was fucking with me again. If the cop who shot himself had only shattered his thighbone, why did the doctor press his stomach? Why did he want to know what the doctors were saying when they didn't even look at his leg? Why does he throw a blanket over his head when the old battleship takes a sample of my blood? Surely the sight of his own blood would be much more unnerving.

Floating into hospital room 9, Julie Christie plopped on the corner of my bunk and patted a cheek. It was too much to lift my head or even acknowledge her presence. On a whim, I zoomed to my place on the TV. "Who looks more like Marilyn Monroe," Ethel asked, "me or Lucy?" Fred looked them both over and said, "I think I look more like Marilyn Monroe."

From my lofty perch, I was able to focus on Julie Christie with much sharper clarity. She was a red-haired angel with hypodermic fingers. When she bent forward I zeroed in on her pleasing butt.

The cop who shot himself said, "Lucky bastard. He gets morphine while I survive on one lousy pill a day." His lips never moved nor did Julie Christie take the slightest notice of his remark. Pinching the skin on my hip, Julie Christie pricked the fold with her finger and spurted hot morphine.

"Why don't they give you a shot?" I asked.

He shrugged. "I caught you eyeballing her butt."

"Why do you settle for one lousy pill a day?"

"What?"

"One lousy pill."

"How do you know?"

"How do I know what?"

He eyeballed me suspiciously. "You're fucking with me again."

"No, I'm not. If you're in pain, why don't they give you more pills or a shot?"

He hesitated. "Kildare says the drugs eat up my stomach."

THIRTEEN
Mountain Slipping

*If you invent a sport,
make certain it makes you bleed.*

It was 3 a.m. on my orange night clock. With a fresh bottle of warm burgundy piss resting on my belly, I fell prey to my vicious brooding again. Leering through the hospital window was the portly Bob's Big Boy, offering a famous triple-decker with fries from the roof of his tacky teen hangout.

"Scram, you gross little shit," I snapped.

Of all the ridiculous accidents!

Harry Kay was dead, though. It was official. Even Dr. Kildare and the cop who shot himself knew he was a stiff in northern Minnesota—or wherever.

Suddenly the TV popped to life. My initial suspicion fell on the cop who shot himself, but the blanket was still tossed over his head and his remote control had long ago been confiscated by the old battleship.

Appearing on the TV screen was an image of Larson's ghostly face. It caught me off guard.

He said, "Kay, don't hide in the timber."

Since the accident, I had nearly forgotten about Larson. Yet I never completely forgot that his bloodied hands were still clamped to my left leg in Hughes Supermarket.

On Maray Point, Larson was peering down at the town of Lake of the Woods, and stretching his legs. He scanned the 27 giant Jeffreys.

"Larson," I said, "don't look in the trees, I'm on the hospital bed."

At the edge of Iris Ridge on Maray Point, with its creepy great southern oak, was the most ideal section on Blue Mountain for mountain slipping. Larson was an expert and one of the originators of the sport.

Springing off Maray Point, Larson sailed twenty-five feet down the slope before splashing into moist dirt and skidding another few yards. His hiking boots transformed into a little surfboard. Shifting his weight, he cut into the ridge and banked off a Jeffrey pine. This time, however, he struck the ground awkwardly and stumbled headfirst into the bush. The yucca brandished their switchblades and slashed his arms.

Swatting the dust off his Levi's, Larson reminded me of the countless times I had tumbled on Blue Mountain and been dragged mercilessly across rock and thorn. His workout possessed the intensity of our senior cross-country campaign. Granada Hills had won the L.A. varsity title in 1964.

As Larson knifed between the Jeffreys, dense as pier pilings, Garrett Kay exploded onto the TV screen roller coasting over his head and kicking up a ten-foot rooster tail of soft dirt.

I said, "Why did you run from me?"
"Just playing the game."
"What game?"
"You know about the game."
"How do I know about the game?"
Larson said, "In Organ Pipe you won."

FOURTEEN
Freedom

*When it comes to wilderness,
rangers don't know shit.*

Under a bruising sky, I coaxed my scruffy Schwinn into an L.A. housing tract behind the San Franciscan apartments in Sepulveda and scouted for J.

My buddies and I had all grown up in a similar bumper-to-bumper tract in the Valley. No doubt the cop who shot himself shared comparable history. None of us frequented the old Granada Hills neighborhood, but my memory of the pranks and antics on Clymer Street was remarkably intense.

At 27, I endured my first nostalgia attack.

San Gabriel winds, however, iced my veins. Leaning on a curb, I glared into the picture window of a particularly cheery home and burned with envy. My thoughts drifted back to the accident. From the floor of Hughes Supermarket, I plotted robbery and mayhem.

When a balding family Dad stepped to the window, I made a threatening sneer. Under my leather coat I pretended to fondle a revolver. "Scare the hell out of the bastard," I said. "Ms. D.'s Seville didn't burst into his comfy existence." But the Dad never flinched. He raised his arm and offered an Olympia beer.

He said, "Just bought a fresh case."

"It's the water."

"In 'Nam, Olympia was king."
"T-shirts must have been the rage too."
"Lakers are on TV."
"Give it to Elgin."

At the corner of Lassen and Haskell, J. was pedaling his clunker toward the Rustic Grill in Granada Hills.

He said, "Hey, Kay, did you know the Lakers are on TV all week? Too bad there's no cable in Organ Pipe."

"Saguaro cactus and cholla can't stop Wilt or Jerry West."

"I talked to Larson this morning," J. said. "He wants to climb Sierra del Ajo."

"Bullfuckingshit."

"He's on a collision course with his fear."

I said, "Dunham is tagging along."

"No premonitions, I hope."

"He promised to keep a low profile."

"You keep an eye on him."

"How was your backpacking trip?"

He frowned. "Intriguing."

"Where'd you camp?"

"Joaquin Murrieta, on Mt. Pinos."

"Good Lord, J., Mt. Pinos is a graveyard with wolves."

"Something weird happened too."

There was a long pause. "I'm listening."

He said, "Not sure if I should tell you."

"Only if it concerns me."

"You want it straight?"

"Sure."

"At dusk, an elderly ranger sauntered into Murrieta on foot."

"On foot?" I shook my head. "Never saw a ranger on Mt. Pinos or Blue, but Los Padres rangers usually pack with horses."

"It was odd, especially when I noticed a double-barreled shotgun under his long gray overcoat."

"Long gray overcoat?"

"He said there are no wolves on Mt. Pinos."

"No wolves? But…"

"The ranger said wolves are extinct in California. Even coyotes refuse to roam Pinos—too dry and windy. 'Red-tails have a shrill scream,' he said. 'Maybe you heard a red-tail.'

" 'It was a wolf,' I said. 'Why can't you accept the idea of a wolf or large canine on Pinos? Just because something hasn't been seen in California or the Los Padres for a few years doesn't mean it no longer exists. Mt. Pinos would make a perfect home for a wolf.'

"The elderly ranger only grinned and reminded me I hadn't *seen* anything. And just because I heard something doesn't mean it's on Mt. Pinos either. He said people have heard voices, bells, and a symphony orchestra on Pinos, but that doesn't prove they exist. 'Bandit shootouts are real popular,' he added.

" 'I heard a wolf,' I insisted. 'My buddy heard it too.'

"The old geezer perked up. 'What's you buddy's name?'

" 'Garrett Kay,' I said, without thinking.

" 'Where is Garrett Kay?'

" 'This is crazy. How did you know I heard a wolf?'

" 'Simple. All backpackers hear wolves on Mt. Pinos.'

"I looked at him closely. 'Hey, you're not a real ranger.' "

As I was zipping along Lassen toward Granada Hills, the temperature on the porch post dropped down to a chilly nine degrees. I was free because I didn't care about anyone or if anyone cared about me. For the moment, I didn't need or blame anyone. Of course J. was by my side, but we were oceans apart.

Rejecting our usual route to Granada Hills, J. turned south at Woodly and I followed. As was my custom, I paid little attention to our direction until I spotted the gothic Veterans Hospital and Baptist High School. This was a dangerous route. At the edge of Woodly Hill, J. braked his clunker and I plowed into his back wheel.

He laughed. "Not paying attention."

"It's not my strong suit."

Woodly Hill was an asphalt roller coaster, legendary in the Valley for its harrowing plunge.

"Check out the streets," J. said. "We're alone."

I pointed down the hill. "Not quite."

At the bottom of Woodly, the Plumber Street intersection was a river of cars
flowing toward Chatsworth and Simi Valley.

J. said, "Let's bet our next moment."

"What?"

"Double or nothing. Make up for the loss on Blue Mountain."

"Or lose another moment."

"Poor attitude, Kay. Let's bet we can coast down Woodly Hill and cross Plumber without getting hammered."

I said, "We can't keep betting our…"

There was a faint howl on the grounds of the gothic Veterans Hospital. My heart froze. It's another wolf, I thought. No, it was the siren from the mental ward warning God and Sepulveda that some unfortunate, ravaged by Vietnam, was escaping via the orange grove

"Fuck it," I growled. "Double or nothing."

Pedaling off the edge of Woodly Hill, we were reckless and bursting with adrenalin. As we skimmed over the road, the asphalt turned smooth and glassy.

At top speed my scruffy Schwinn shook furiously and veered into J. Our wheels tapped. Suddenly the remaining stretch of Woodly Hill transformed into Maray Point on Iris Ridge. Helplessly I jammed the brakes. As I hurtled off Maray point, my left hand reached out and whacked the great southern oak.

Bucking in the dirt, my Schwinn crunched through brittle manzanita, narrowly dodging Jeffrey and piñón pine. At the bottom of Iris Ridge the signal at Plumber turned red. Instead of being frightened, I was exhilarated.

As I soared across Plumber, the traffic screeched and parted like the Red Sea,
followed by a chorus of honks and profanity. Catapulting over my handlebars, I tumbled into the Busch Gardens parking lot.

I said, "Watch the curb."

Sliding on his backside, J. imitated Maury Wills stealing second base. He raised his fist and shouted, "Double or nothing, Kay. We won our next moment back from Blue Mountain."

"Trot over to the 7-11 and buy some chardonnay."

"To toast our freedom in the Valley."

I said, "Dab our wounds too."

FIFTEEN
Yosemite

If your watch stops, that does not necessarily mean you are dead.

Flopping his pack next to a weathered sign reading, *For Experienced Climbers Only*, Dunham leaned on a bristlecone pine and squinted at the granite spine of Half Dome. Near its summit, two metal cables dangled precariously, stretching four hundred feet to our packs.

He said, "I'm nauseous. You forgot to mention it was the Empire State Building."

"It's steeper than I remember," I admitted.

"Christ, Kay."

"It's changed since 1964."

"People change, not Half Dome."

"Guess I fucked up."

The sun was behind El Capitan. Dunham said, "I'm camping at Nevada Falls. Too late for an assault."

I said, "Not necessarily." A large shadow inched up Half Dome's spine. "Sun is barely retreating."

Dunham eyeballed Half Dome. "The eight-mile hike was brutal. Don't expect me to climb Godzilla in the dark."

"Relax, Dun. Let's drink some water and discuss it. Do you see the shadow line on Half Dome?"

"No, you don't. I know what you're thinking. Only J. is pretentious enough to race a sunset."

"It's only sport, Dun."

"J. can be out of control, Kay."

I took hold of a cable. "We'll have sweaty palms, but it'll be a grand assault."

"Include successful."

"Have you ever dreamed about Half Dome?"

"I'm not listening."

I said, "Good Lord, Dun. Look."

Mist had crept up from Merced Lake and obscured our packs.

Dunham said, "Son of a bitch. Now we've got to climb. This damp shit will ruin our trade."

"Take the lead. If you slip I can break your fall, or tumble with you."

"I can see it in the *L.A. Times.*"

With a firm grip on the cables, I dug my right boot into the granite. It stuck to the dome like a barnacle. Dunham began to clamber up the wall, stretching for each chunk of cable with his long arms. After a hundred feet or so, we were both wasted. Fitting my heel into a large crack, I braced against the wall and dropped the lines.

"I'm crippled, Kay."

I said, "Don't feel like the Lone Ranger. We're climbing too fast." Cotton mouth pasted my throat. "No need to sprint in this fucking altitude. We need to establish a pace. Remember, we're over eight thousand feet."

Unzipping his pack, Dunham handed me a plastic bottle. After several gulps,
water gushed over my chin and down my chest.

"It's only water, Kay, not chardonnay."

"You talk like Larson."

"Set the pace. If I start to fall I'll grab your ankles."

Chalking my palms, I noticed we had climbed out of the mist and were perched just above the clouds. It was like looking out the window of a jet plane. Huge luminous pillows camouflaged our dizzy loftiness and blocked the decadent sights of urban Yosemite Valley. Less than one hundred feet above my head was the sun line.

"Coming to get ya," I whispered.

At the end of the cables, a tired old ray of sun touched my cheek. "Ladies first," I said, stepping aside and allowing Dunham to bask in the sun's final glimmer.

Tromping to the edge, which had a four-thousand-foot vertical drop, I dangled my legs and watched the sky redden. It had cleared up. Lights and campfires twinkled in Yosemite Valley.

"Did you get it?" Dunham asked.

"Yeah, did you?"

"Yeah."

"Fantastic. Let's do it *aqui*."

Our special plan had been to make an exchange on Half Dome in Yosemite. Rummaging in the pack, I retrieved my petrified rock from Organ Pipe National Monument while Dunham popped the cork of a bottle of chardonnay.

Legs still dangling off the edge, we spread our wares. Two leather coats, an old army blanket, a Coleman Peak-1, three steaks, aluminum pan, rolls and butter, Spanish olives, and Red Rooster work gloves. Quite possibly Dunham was the only person in our solar system to store milk in a canteen. As he washed down four codeine pills, I chopped my cocaine into two thick lines. After a quick snort with my worn fifty-dollar bill, I took a long draw on the chardonnay.

"Why do you use milk with your codeine?"

"Coats the stomach."

"I'll store a mental note."

Angry black clouds churned over Tioga Pass and rolled in the sky toward Half Dome.

"Let's set up the gear and cook dinner."

Dunham said, "Pardon me if I only observe."

"What's wrong?"

"Not sure if I can walk."

"Don't fret," I said, sniffling. "It's my passion to fix a proper meal, delicious with a touch of artistry. Too many Henry Miller novels, I suppose."

"My trip down may be calamitous."

"Mr. Peppy will guide you."

"No doubt. You've been grinding your teeth for twenty minutes."

"It's silly to hike all the way back to Nevada Falls tonight. I'll slide down and get our mummy bags."

"In the dark?"

"I've got a flashlight. What else do we need?"

"*Nada*. But if I think of something I'll yell."

"Just be certain I'm not on my way back up."

"We may be in for some weather."

"Hey, Dun, what time is it?"

Dunham glanced at his new watch. "Damn, my new watch stopped."

"Then you're dead," I said. "Twilight zone."

"All mangled up and you're still a wiseass."

Guided by the moon, I descended quickly and shot right back up. As I neared the end of the cables, Dunham shined his flashlight in my face. "Did you remember the chocolate bars?" he yelled.

"Fuck," I yelled back.

"I knew I'd think of something."

He was slurring his words so I decided to play a trick. "What time is it?" I said, fully aware that in his stupor he had forgotten what had been said earlier.

"Damn," he said, equally distressed. "My new watch stopped."

"Then you're dead. Twilight zone."

As I reached the end of the cable, he said, "You're a real Groucho tonight, Kay." I handed him the chocolate bars.

Tipping the second bottle of chardonnay into our cups, I chewed the wrapper off my chocolate bar and bit a corner. It melted slowly on the tip of my tongue.

I said, "Organ Pipe in two weeks."

Dunham pounced on the opportunity. "No one has ever told me. How did it happen? Why the big mystery?"

I said, "Okay, but it's only my version. It was early morning. On the way up Sierra del Ajo, Larson wanted to sit on a ledge and enjoy the desert. There wasn't enough room for us all, so he insisted we go up without him. Insulted us too.

"At the top I began to fix breakfast. When J. went to the edge to check on him, he was lying on his back next to our leather coats. He didn't make a sound. He just fell sixty feet and neither of us saw or heard it happen. 'Nothing I'd want to hear,' J. said.

"Scooping him off the rocks, I noticed there wasn't a mark on him, but he was suffering from severe internal bleeding. J. and I lugged him two miles back to my battered 340 Duster. Struggling with the legs, I had a clear view of his face. He was conscious but very pale and aloof.

"At the Duster he looked at me and said, 'I'm slipping, Garrett.' I said, "No, Larson, you're winning. You're still alive.' He smiled and said, 'I'm still in contention.' "

Dunham had passed out, but the chocolate remained on my tongue. Balled up in my mummy bag, I counted the seconds between wind gusts. 25, 26, 27—WHOOOSH! Rehashing our ordeal at Organ Pipe left me spooked and restless.

The TV jumped to life with an image of the cold and empty streets at Yosemite Market. At 10 p.m. a burgundy van steered into the parking lot and pulled beside me. Bob Dylan blared on the stereo. When I opened the door, Julie Christie's teeth glowed from the dash lights. In her lap was a jug of vodka sunstrokes.

She said, "This will kill the chill. I think I mixed it too strong."

"Quite improbable."

Out popped my razor blade and petrified rock from Organ Pipe National Monument. I said, "Nice song." When she noticed my chopping ritual, she appeared
anxious but said nothing.

"Let's cruise, Christie."

"Why do you call me Christie?"

"You resemble Julie Christie in the movie *McCabe and Mrs. Miller*."

"I've never heard of it."

"It's a cult classic." I glanced around. "Drive into the campground."

Squeezing into a vacant site, she turned down the stereo and slipped into the back of the van. A green Girl Scout sleeping bag lay unzipped in the corner.

She said, "Still cold?" Her eyes were Girl Scout green.

"It's heating up."

While I curled my worn fifty-dollar bill, Julie Christie poured another sunstroke. "I'm amazed you remembered our date," she said. "It's a sweet compliment, of course, but you seemed way too drunk in Canoga Park to remember me and a Yosemite rendezvous."

"Hardly."

"But you were drunk."

"No, I didn't drink at the party. A buddy tricked me into swallowing four codeine pills."

"Codeine not your style?"

"Puts my stomach on a roller coaster."

"Try taking them with milk."

I said, "You are the second person to tell me that."

"Where do you live?"

"San Francisco Apartments in Sepulveda. But I'm moving to Lake of the Woods."

"Is that the town near Frazier Park?"

"Yeah, at the base of Blue Mountain."

"Did you say Blue Mountain? Isn't that mountain called…?

"Locals call it Blue."

She brushed my hand with slender fingers that were hot and moist. My arm slipped over her shoulder and I smelled her hair.

I said, "Aren't you a brain surgeon or something?"

She giggled. "RN at Valley Memorial in Van Nuys."

"You look too young to be an RN."

"I'm twenty-seven."

"Really? Me too."

"What do you do at twenty-seven?"

"Nothing much."

"Tell me," she said.

"Well, hike the Tehachapi's, watch old movies, and read Henry Miller."

"What about work?"

"Nail up patio roofs with Larson."

She unbuttoned my bandana shirt and slid a moist finger in circles on my chest. Inside her green Girl Scout sleeping bag our bodies brushed. When she kissed me on the mouth her hips began to stir.

Chopping a fine hill on my petrified rock, I cut four lines with the razor blade and handed her my worn fifty-dollar bill. We had both nearly fallen asleep, but were quickly seduced by the boost.

"Is this your first visit to Yosemite?"

"I was here in 1964."

"Excellent," she said, handing me the keys to the van. "Let's do an after hours tour of the valley."

"Wait a minute," I said, dusting off my petrified rock from Organ Pipe National Monument. "Let's do two more."

As the morning sun skirted the eastern Sierras, I rolled up my mummy bag and battled the October chill on Half Dome with a tin of hot mud. For some reason, I slid my knife from its sheath and began shooting imaginary bandits on the rocks.

"What are you doing, Loco Loco?" the cop who shot himself asked, sitting on his bed near my Coleman Peak-1.

"Don't know," I said. My head was still woozy from bandits and shootouts, Margaritas and women. "A posse or something was chasing me through the Tehachapi's. In the end…" I struggled, but couldn't form my words.

Dunham said, "In the end you fired your gun along a creek."

He stunned me. "How did you know?"

Dunham slid out his knife and shot me. "I was at the creek too."

"Did I shoot you?"

"Only you can recall."

"Why?"

"Because it's yours."

"What's mine?"

"The dream, of course."

SIXTEEN
Monopoly

*Friends who fuck with each
other can still be friends.*

Headlights from a diesel truck flooded our campsite on Half Dome, tracing the window frame of my hospital room on its granite spine.

"Saddle up, Dun," I said from the perimeter.

"Dream is over, Kay."

On the deserted streets, the truck veered onto Sherman Way from Van Nuys Boulevard and rumbled toward the San Diego Freeway. Its violent revs jarred the hospital brick all the way up to my IV. Thankfully morphine still thumped sluggishly through my veins.

It was 3 a.m. on my orange night clock. Time to piss. Lifting the plastic bottle between the safety bars, I bent Little Kay into its spout and blasted a hardy stream of urine. Capping the bottle, I set the warm contents on my belly and contemplated.

It's bliss not to know better, I decided. But surely by now there were no more traces of blood. I gritted my teeth and tapped the overhead lamp.

Larson's secret war on Sierra del Ajo raged out of control. Weathering a series of ambushes, I concentrated on the girls I had fucked until an image appeared on the TV.

Garrett Kay was waiting on the cold and empty front steps at the Yosemite market. At 10:00 p.m. a burgundy van steered into the parking lot and pulled beside me. "Early one morning the sun was shining, I was laying in bed," said the stereo. When I opened the door, Julie Christie's teeth glowed from the dash lights. In her lap was a...

Astonishingly, I had sprung an erection. Giggling with delight, I squeezed it with my fingers to make certain it was real. If I could manage an erection, I couldn't be bleeding to death.

At last I remembered the cop who shot himself and his reaction to the previous time I had fooled with the lights.

In the darkness, I said, "You awake?"

"What do you think, Loco Loco?" His overhead lamp snapped to life.

"I knew you'd be waiting," I said. "Sorry about the music."

"No problem, I like Dylan. Besides, it's another restless night."

"How come?"

"My stomach hurts. I need more pills. Plus, you were yapping about the hide and go seek nonsense."

"Say anything new?"

"Nope."

"Ever try milk with your codeine?"

"What for?"

"It coats the stomach."

He cocked his head. "I'll ask Kildare. Thanks."

"Did you hear a truck?"

He looked at me. "You've never heard the big rigs? They visit every night. I like to listen because they're going places and I'm not. But don't change the subject. I know the score. You took a piss and wondered if there was blood in the bottle." He hesitated. "I can see the red streaks from here."

"True, but I got an erection."

71

"A what?"

"Boner."

He said, "I get it. I fuck with you so you fuck with me. All mangled up and you're still a wiseass."

"Let's try something new."

"Like what?"

I said, "Let's not fuck with each other."

"What do you mean?"

"Only for an hour. Don't feel threatened."

"I'm not following."

"Let's play a game. I ask you a question and you ask me a question, but when we answer we don't fuck with each other."

He squinted his eyes. "Why?"

"So we can be friends."

He said, "We are friends, aren't we?"

"We're friends who can't help each other."

"What are you up to, Loco Loco?"

"I ask you a question and you ask me a question, but when we answer we don't fuck with each other."

"What the hell? I'll do anything to make you quit fucking with the lights."

"Want to go first?"

He said, "No, it's your play. Ask the question."

"What happened on the morning you shot yourself?"

"Christ, Kay." He looked uncomfortable. "I already told you."

"You lied."

"Maybe I did, but it's none of your business."

"It's my question."

"I'm not sure I can explain."

"Try."

"It's personal."

"Goddamn it. Do you want to play or not? I know you are dying to ask me a question."

"Okay, but I don't like it. On the other hand, you might be impressed."

"Impressed?"

"My little gun play was nothing but a scam gone awry."

"You already lied about this shit."

"It was a scam, nothing but a little scam."

"You're making no sense."

"Last month the Department issued new nine-millimeter handguns. Sweet piece. But I immediately noticed there was a problem with my safety. The latch was loose and slipped out of position. As I was about to fix it, I thought, what if while I'm putting my pants on the safety slips and a bullet accidentally discharges into my thigh? It would smart, but visualize the lawsuits and disability checks. Think of all the time and money to realize my dreams."

"Which are?"

"That's private."

"Crapola."

"You don't understand, Kay. With a dab of blood, my financial stability is secure."

"You're telling me you shot yourself in the thigh on purpose?"

"Just a little nick."

"Nick? You practically blew off your leg. Hit an artery, I'm told, and nearly bled to death."

"Slight exaggeration. When you pursue the perfect scam you need an extra dollop of blood.

Besides the gun manufacturer, I'll sue the Department and win a lifetime pension."

"You used hollow point bullets."

"Messy little bastards."

"Stop it."

"Stop what?"

I said, "You're fucking with me. You're still fucking with me."

"What are you talking about?"

"You didn't try to nick yourself any more than I jumped in front of the Seville. You can't stand the sight of blood. I've seen you turn white when the old battleship takes my sample. No way you could sit calmly in your living room and watch the blood flow. The doctors whisper in the hall and you beg to know what they're saying. You're jealous because I get a shot while you're only allowed one lousy pill a day. There's something wrong with your gut, not just your leg. Why can't you stop fucking with me?"

The cop who shot himself sighed heavily. "Someone needs to get over his obsession with me."

"Tell me."

"No."

"You owe me."

"It's too stupid."

"So are the lies."

"You won't like the part that includes you."

"Tell me everything."

He frowned. "You and I are in the same fucked up condition. That's why they put us together in room nine."

"What condition?"

"Terminal condition, Loco Loco. I'm dying too. It'll be interesting to see which of us expires first. Expires. That's how Kildare describes going stiff. Kildare has a mean poker face. While you were sleeping, I heard him say in the hall that the next twelve to twenty-four hours were critical, for both of us."

"What is this drivel?"

"Internal bleeding, man. We're pissing ourselves to death."

"This isn't happening. I feel fine."

"You're on morphine, Kay. Try going it with no medication."

"You admit your stomach is fucked up?"

"You play hide and go seek in a desert I can't find on a map while I pretend to have shot myself in the leg for a scam. What a pair." He banged his overhead lamp.

"Sorry I fucked with you. You're a good friend and didn't deserve it. You've earned the right to hear the truth."

"Only wanted you to stop fucking with me."

He said, "No, I owe you. My shooting was just a ridiculous accident played out the exact way I told you earlier with a missing piece or two. While I was putting my pants on, with my new nine-millimeter and its slippery safety, the widow missed her floor again and passed my kitchen window. But this time she pounded on the door. Never before had she knocked. It startled me and forced my hand to bump my fucking gun. The blast was ear shattering.

"Now here's the part I left out of the original story. The bullet ricocheted off my thighbone, severed the artery, and slashed through my stomach and intestines. Add runny shit to the blood, urine, and vomit I sloshed in waiting for the ambulance. Apparently killed the widow's Labrador downstairs too."

"What happened to the widow?"

He shrugged. "Guess she ran like hell back to her apartment. Later, upon discovering her dead Labrador, I heard her shriek 'Wooo-Deee.' It was chilling."

"You never told me the dog's name was Woody."

"Now I shit blood and can't eat solid food. There's so much internal injury, I see blood in my sweat. Kildare knows I'm dying but won't level with me. I lied about the shooting because I'm slipping and have no control. Or so I thought. Until you were wheeled into room nine, I had surrendered to my expiration. Yet you are unfathomable, Kay. You're fearless. You refuse to acknowledge your own imminent death, and you're a wiseass."

"Me?"

"You've made me believe in myself. We can both beat our accidents and live."

His confession was astounding. "I'm going to live, I think."

He said, "It's my turn, Kay."

"It finally makes sense."

"What about my question?"

"What question?"

"The game. You ask me a question and I ask you a question and we don't fuck with each other."

"The widow must have been driving Woody to Henry the dog vet. Thanks for not fucking with me."

"May I ask my question?"

"Ask it."

"What are you hiding from me? Don't you dare deny it."

I had anticipated his question and decided to give it to him straight. "This will not be pretty, but it's important that you know."

"Know what?"

"I didn't want to tell you she died."

"Who died?"

"Ms. D."

"Who is Ms. D.?"

"She's the widow who's Labrador you accidentally shot in the head."

"How do you know her name?"

"We met."

"You met the widow from my apartment building?"

"Sort of."

"How do you know she died?"

"She crashed into Hughes Supermarket with her black Seville."

"WHAT?"

"The widow Ms. D. knocked me into a freezer."

He shuddered. "No, you're fucking with me."

"No, I'm not."

"Don't fuck with me, Kay. I was honest with you."

"She swerved to miss an empty shopping cart and crashed into Hughes Supermarket."

"No way."

"Ms. D. is the widow from your apartment building."

"This is not happening."

I said, "Woody was in the front seat of the car."

"What else did the Seville do in Hughes?"

"Demolished cash register nine and knocked Dunham into a shelf of chili beans."

"What happened to your buddy J.?"

"I'm not sure. Glass rained into his face and then he was gone."

He said, "Christ, you were talking about the accident in your sleep."

"No, I dreamed about Halloween."

"Halloween?"

"We played a game on Halloween in Organ Pipe National Monument."

"Are you certain the widow died?"

"Larson pulled her out of the Seville and dumped her on the floor. When he backed the car out of the ice cream freezer, I fell on top of her and couldn't move. Trust me, she was a stiff."

"What happened to Larson?"

I had to reflect for a moment. "Nothing. Ms. D. missed him. He's still holding onto my leg. I need a drink."

The cop who shot himself got a funny twinkle in his eye. "You won't believe what my wife brought this afternoon," he said, sliding a bottle of chardonnay from his night table. "Do you play Monopoly? Drink up and let's play a game. Do you like this wine?"

"Where's my glass?"

SEVENTEEN
Halloween 1974

*In Organ Pipe National Monument,
Kay wins the game.*

Throughout our entire dinner, J. had been studying the arms of a giant saguaro, occasionally reaching out and touching its barbed thorns with his fingertips. As a red sun sank behind Sierra del Ajo, he popped the cork on another bottle of chardonnay.

He said, "This will be our finest game."

I looked up. "It's freezing."

"Why is J. so pale?"

Dunham said, "Same with you, Kay." Our breath hung in the air.

"Children of the night," Larson said.

"BelaFuckingLarson."

"Maybe J. is really Roman Polanski."

"Or Sharon somebody."

Crouching near our tents, J. slid out his rubber-killing knife and sketched the giant saguaro in the dirt. Its arms pointed to the four directions.

He said, "Choose an arm and follow its course until you are alone." In the dusk, J. began to stroll in a westerly direction.

"*Adios, bandido,*" I said.

"Keep an eye over your shoulder, Kay."

"What for?"

"It's the game." He handed me the bottle of chardonnay. "In the game everything is a trick."

Selecting the southern arm, I stepped back so Larson and Dunham could decide. J. had quickly wandered into an orange haze. When Larson erased the sketch with his hiking boot, I took a deep draw of air from the empty bottle.

I tossed the bottle to the ground. "Damn. I fell for the dead-bottle trick."

"Dunham shook his head. "J. and his silly games."

"It's just for fun."

"I'm not sure I want to play."

Larson said, "I wouldn't care to be the only star again."

When a player lost sight of the other three, the game was officially in session. Stalk the others and take them out with your rubber killing knife. From my vantage point, Larson was the last to drop out of sight. Lingering in the orange mist, he went behind the giant saguaro and stepped into a cholla grove. The advantage was clearly mine. Slipping into a dry riverbed, I checked his tracks and circled behind him.

"This is almost too easy," I said, which instinctively put me on guard. In the cholla grove, however, Larson had faded into the mist. Be wary of the backtrack, I reminded myself. It had been a clever trick at Butterscotch Creek.

Crouching under the cholla, game paranoia got the best of me. At any moment my best friends could be in close proximity, yet we were oceans apart.

Without warning my brooding returned in earnest. It was depressing to acknowledge Harry Kay was no longer in northern Minnesota. I desperately needed company. I wanted to rock climb with Larson and J., or make a trade with Dunham. It was the hour for a campfire.

I shouted, "Time out." My cry was answered by silence. If I attempted to cancel the game, my friends would only believe it was a trick. In the game everything was a trick. Sinking deeper into the cholla, I waited for Hughes Supermarket to recede. Sierra del Ajo, with its jagged teeth, was eyeballing me.

From enemy territory, an object whistled over my head and landed in the bush. There was no other movement in the vicinity. Walking point, I spotted what I believed to be a mirror or piece of glass in the sand. It was someone's rubber killing knife, only this knife was an authentic Buckhorn with a stainless steel blade.

"Good Lord."

Reeking of iced seafood, wind swirled up the dry riverbed and ruffled my hair. I counted the interval. 25, 26, 27—WHOOOSH! A sprinkle of rain spattered my face.

From a distance, I noticed the top of our giant saguaro. This tree resembled no other in Organ Pipe. The cactus had been altered. Its trunk had a deep slash and the western arm that J. had followed was severed and missing in action. A chill ran up the back of my neck. From a safe distance, I conducted a thorough investigation of the perimeter. On the other side of the mutilated trunk, long black hair was blowing in the rainy wind.

I said, "Don't care to know what's on the backside of that saguaro."

"Walk point, Loco Loco," the cop said.

"It's bliss not to know better."

He said, "Don't be a chickenshit."

In a wide arc I pushed between the thickets and tumbleweeds, making certain I remained hidden from the giant saguaro. On the back wall of Hughes Supermarket, I found the directory. Garden Plants and Cacti—Aisle 15.

The cop said, "What is it?"

"No clue."

"Move in closer."

On the backside of the giant saguaro, J. was stuck on the spines with his throat painted red. His breath puffed into the crisp air. My hand covered my mouth.

The cop said, "Who painted his throat?"

"How did it happen? There was no sound."

"Nothing I'd want to hear."

Looking on the ground, I said, "J., where did all the broken glass come from?"

"Stand back, Garrett," he said. "I'm fine."

"What happened?"

"It's the game."

"Don't talk crazy."

"We're still struggling with Hughes Supermarket."

"Let me help you down."

"No, Garrett, let go. Leave me." When he saw the hurt look in my eyes, he said, "I'm sorry, Garrett. Don't worry about me. You still have ice cream smeared on your Levi's. It's only the game."

"J.," I stammered. "Who painted your neck?"

"Listen to me, Kay. He's here in Organ Pipe. He must cover a huge district."

"Who?"

"You'll meet him."

"What am I supposed to do?"

He said, "It's only the game, Kay. Nick me on the throat and find Larson and Dunham. I've already lost. You can win."

"Why should I nick you on the throat?"

"Because the glass cut me in the accident. Plus I tore the buttons off your leather coat."

I looked. The buttons were indeed missing from my leather coat. "How can I nick you with a rubber blade?"

"Do it, Kay."

When I slid out my knife its blade was stainless steel. "This isn't happening."

"Do it."

"Who is here in Organ Pipe?" But he refused to speak. When I aimed my knife at his throat, L.A.'s Balboa and Devonshire trembled. Slivers of Hughes plate window rained into the supermarket, whistling over my head and shattering on the floor and counters.

The blade slipped from my hand. "Holy shit."

J. said, "Pick it up. Kay. Finish the game."

My battered 340 Duster was parked near our tents. Tumbling into another riverbed, I shut my eyes and waved the blade murderously in the air. Pressing against the dusty bank, perspiration dripped off my chin and stung my left arm. Didn't need to look to know my skin had been gashed by the cholla. With two fingers, I smeared the blood over my arm.

I looked at Dr. Kildare. "Don't mind admitting I'm terrified."

He said, "It's fear that keeps you on the edge."

Hugging the right bank for cover, I spotted Larson strutting boldly across the desert flats. Not within range of a toss, however. I strained my neck to see if there was a trace of red paint on his rubber killing knife, but he was visible only from the waist up. No way Larson or Dunham would paint a red line on J.'s neck. Who then? Quickly, I checked my own knife.

When I looked up, Larson had vanished. Tracing his exact route was an elderly man dressed in a Los Padres National Forest ranger uniform with a long gray overcoat. The image of this vaguely familiar spook was so incredibly stunning I stumbled backwards and landed squarely on my ass.

Garrett Kay had had enough! Leaping to my feet, I scampered to the 340 Duster with all stealth hurled to the wolves. Sticking my hand in the window, I pawed the ignition, but the key had been removed. I slapped the steering wheel and the horn honked.

I shouted, "Who swiped my Duster key?"

Lying on the front seat was a double-barreled shotgun with the Duster key taped to the second trigger. Clearly a choice was being offered, or challenge. My first impulse was to fire up the 340 engine and bolt for L.A. But I couldn't abandon my friends. Plus, the game was exhilarating. Dropping the key into my left boot, I lifted the clumsy shotgun and re-entered the Organ Pipe.

Jokes began to pour off my tongue. "Am I high or is this how it feels to die?" The x-ray man chuckled. "Hey," I shouted in a hoarse voice. Slipping across the border ditch into Mexico, the

word ricocheted off the Sonoran Mountains and exploded back into
Arizona. "Stick a chili bean up your dick."

Dunham appeared with his back to me. He seemed to be retreating from something further up the riverbed. When he was finally satisfied, he turned and saw me with the gun.

"G. Kay."

I let the shotgun fall to the ground. "You were right, Dun. J. and his silly games."

"No, Kay, you were right. He's tough."

"Am I high or is this how it feels to die?"

Dunham smiled. "Either way you should know."

"What are you doing?"

"Hiding from the game. What about you?"

"Not sure."

He said, "You should play."

"Why not you?"

"It's not my style."

I looked at Sierra del Ajo. "If you don't play the game, what are you going to do?"

"Lose, of course."

"What does that mean?"

"Remember our night on Half Dome? We dreamed about bandits and shootouts, booze and women." I nodded. "That's when I quit. We traded places."

Vaguely I remembered the dream. There had been booze and women, and a gunfight at Sespe Creek. When I looked at Dunham, his eyes were shut and the lines on his face had deepened. He looked twenty-seven years old.

I said, "Whatever you're doing, stop it."

"Hey, Kay. Do you have a couple of pills? You never fail to bring me a couple of pills."

Brushing my top pocket, I shook the pill container. "How many do you want?"

"I'll take four."

"Happy birthday, Dun."

"Is that milk in your canteen?"

"Chardonnay."

"Thanks, anyway."

Dipping into his Levi's pocket, he tossed me a small manila envelope. On all fours, he took a drink from the river that had mysteriously filled with rushing water.

"Black Seville has definitely hopped the tracks," he said, pointing over my shoulder.

With a tremendous splash, a shelf of chili beans cascaded into the water. Dunham vanished. Plunging into the river, I groped beneath the freezing surface but couldn't locate his body. An empty shopping cart hopped the bank and slammed into the back of the Seville.

I yelled, "Larson, help me find Dunham."

But Larson wouldn't come.

EIGHTEEN
Green Glass

Kay has a major crush on Julie Christie.

Canceling the morning blood samples. Julie Christie scooped me into a wheelchair and pushed it to the lobby. Twice along the way she combed the left side of my hair with her moist fingers. Glancing over my shoulder, I smiled gratefully.

As a Valley Hospital RN, Julie Christie was responsible for the care and well-being of her patients. Yet even the cop who shot himself admitted she catered to me like an anxious girlfriend.

In the lonely corridor I wished to express my feelings for her, but lacked the confidence to speak with affection. At the main desk, a nasty clerk shoved a wad of papers into my lap.

I said, "What's this?"

The nasty clerk growled. "Sign the papers, Mr. Kay. Don't be such a wiseass."

"What am I signing?"

"Permission."

"Permission for what?"

"Permission to be on your own."

It dawned on me that something unusual was occurring. "What are you doing with my leather coat and Red Rooster work gloves?"

"You're leaving Valley Hospital."

"Is something wrong?"

She said, "On the contrary. Your charts indicate you've recovered."

"Recovered? It's only been a few days."

"More deserving patients need your bed."

"But my internal bleeding and..."

The nasty clerk interrupted with a big sigh. "After he removed your stitches and IV's, Dr. Kildare decided to release you in the morning. He said you've recovered."

"This is ridiculous."

"What you need is fresh air and exercise."

"I can't walk."

"You were walking around Sierra del Ajo."

"You're as goofy as Larry, Moe, and Curly Joe. I'm still pissing blood."

"Recovered," she repeated. "You still need fresh air and exercise."

I said, "I demand to speak with Dr, Kildare."

"I'll give you his home phone number. You can call him from your cabin in Lake of the Woods. What's the name of that big mountain?"

"Blue."

"No, that's not it."

"Locals call it Blue."

"Don't fuck with me, Mr. Kay."

I looked at her closely. "Hey, you're the crabby cashier from Hughes Supermarket."

In the elevator, Julie Christie tapped the basement button. I said, "My cabin in Lake of the Woods is eighty miles from Valley Hospital."

She kissed my forehead. "Your battered 340 Duster is parked at the main exit."

I tested my leg. "My 340 Duster has a clutch."

"Be resourceful."

"I'm not prepared to leave," I said firmly.

"You signed your release papers."

"She tricked me."

"Who?"

"The crabby cashier."

She leaned over to whisper. "Listen to me, Garrett. Dr. Kildare said the outcome was in your hands."

"What does that mean?"

"It means that only you can control what happens, depending on how much you care."

"Of course I care."

"But how badly? Care is more than a word. You must will yourself to stay alive, and never quit."

"What exactly are we talking about?"

"When you need me the most, I will appear."

"No one gave me a chance to say goodbye to the cop who shot himself. I don't even know his name."

"His name is Dan."

"Dan?"

She said, "Dan went into abdominal surgery fifteen minutes ago. His prognosis is very dim.

"We never finished our game of Monopoly. Of course, he was mopping the board with me."

"When you need him, he'll still be lying next to you in a hospital bed."

"There's something I want to tell you, Julie, though now may not be the best time."

"Then save it. I have a good idea."

At the main exit, I was overwhelmed by the dazzling sunshine. My battered 340 Duster was parked in the driveway blocking several ambulances. The lead ambulance honked, but I couldn't see a driver. Julie Christie wheeled me to the driver's side and caressed my shoulder.

She blew me a kiss. "Never forget Yosemite."

I said, "Why don't you stick around?"

She ran to the doors and slipped into the hospital's green glass without looking back.

PART TWO

NINETEEN
Lillian's Music Store

The only way to drink a civilized Margarita is with no ice.

The bandits were whoring at Lillian's Music Store on Sespe Creek in Ojai. Two pianos and a fiddle cranked out a frenzied cowboy tune. Lillian's was packed with gamblers and prairie bums, pickpockets, cowpokes, greasers, businessmen, bushwhackers, and Indians. Also dancers, harlots, ladies, drinking girls, and stoned Chinese.

In an upstairs loft I had fooled with a working girl while pretending she was Julie Christie. Though her prettiness was only slightly tarnished, she was bed-worn and wouldn't kiss me. Afterwards, I stumbled downstairs and ordered a Margarita.

"No ice, please."

The homely bartender said, "Suits me. Pain in the ass to crack ice."

Dunham was chugging his second Singapore Sling. Draining his glass, he watched J. play five-card draw. A young Chicano girl from Canoga Park sat on J.'s lap and pouted. J. was winning at cards, but not without some surly grumbling.

Dunham said, "He's on a roll."

"It all began on Woodly Hill," J. said.

"In "Nam?"

"No, Sepulveda."

"Stakes are too high, J.," I said.

"Look at the bucks, Kay." He flopped a huge roll in my lap. "Pour another round for the table and my friends," he said to the homely bartender. "Pour one for yourself."

The bartender said, "I'll pour my drink, thank you, after I deliver a message."

"What message?"

"Bounty hunter paid me a twenty-dollar gold piece to deliver a message to the winner at cards."

I said, "Twenty-dollar gold piece. Must be an important message."

"Not to me."

J. said, "You look exactly like Elvira's assistant on Channel Nine's Fright Night."

"Hell you say."

"What do you think, Kay?"

I grinned. "J. is correct. You're a spitting image of Dr. Paul Bearer."

The homely bartender bristled with scorn. "You boys from Clymer Street are a pack of wiseasses."

"What do you know about Clymer Street?"

"Walk to the front porch with your hands up and you won't be killed."

"Hell you say," J. mimicked.

"That's the message. He's giving you three minutes."

I said, "What does he want with us?"

"Bounty on your heads. Heard you boys trashed Hughes Supermarket in Granada Hills." He leaned forward and whispered, "Use the back door at the end of the hall. You can escape by following Sespe Creek."

"Why would you help us?" I asked suspiciously. "Bounty hunter might blame you if we escaped."

"Just trying to even the odds, I suppose."

"He's setting us up to be bushwhacked."

"Not me. Much as I dislike you, I don't side with the law."

"It's three against one and he doesn't like the odds."

J. said, "Mix our drinks, barman. You're out of your league."

"Look, friend. He paid me a twenty-dollar gold piece to deliver a message, and I did. I don't know his plans. Maybe he's playing a game."

My double-barreled shotgun wasn't loaded. "I'll check the perimeter."

J. said, "Don't humor him, Kay. He's playing an old bar trick to get rid of us."

"Not very amusing."

"Larson is still upstairs," Dunham said.

J. shouted, "Hey, which one of you is the bounty hunter?" No one in Lillian's looked up.

"In two minutes we'll know," Dunham said, glancing at his new watch.

"Listen, you old spook," J. said, "I'll pay you two twenty-dollar gold pieces to point him out."

"No way, he'd kill me for sure. But he's not sitting among the regulars."

I said, "How can we trust him?"

"I didn't take your gold pieces or the drink."

"Take the fucking drink."

"Let's find Larson and take my 340 Duster."

J. said, "I'm not going to be run out by Dr. Paul Bearer. I want another drink. May
want to go upstairs with my girl again. Besides, I'm winning at cards. He's fucking with us."

The Chicano girl from Canoga Park leaned on the piano and pouted.

Dunham said, "I'm not certain."

"Certain of what?"

"Bad vibes here. Lillian's reminds me of a dream."

"What dream?"

"Not sure. Kay remembers."

J. leaned closer to me. "Jesus, he's scary. Do you ever think about Sierra del Ajo?"

"Only every day."

"Wish he'd keep it to himself."

I said, "I'm stressed too. Where's Larson?"

"You want to check upstairs?"

"Too late."

Dunham said, "One minute. Let's hit the back door."

"Did we use the back door in your dream, Dun?"

"Sarcasm is not your suit, Kay."

"Shut up, both of you. Let's find Larson."

I said, "Bartender didn't mention Larson. Give him a buck and he'll tell Larson what happened. Larson didn't have a mark on him."

"Fifteen seconds," Dunham said.

J. scanned the room once more. "Okay, do it. Move."

Scrambling behind the bar, we raced down a short hallway and kicked out a locked door.

J. said, "Fan out into the trees and ambush the bastard. Kay can nail him with that shotgun."

"Time," Dunham said.

I said, "Let's huddle at Sespe Creek."

As I stomped my L.L. Bean hiking boots on the wooden steps, the orange porch light popped to life.

95

Temperature on the porch post was uncommonly cold for November—nine degrees.

Under a weak glow from the owl-shade lamp, the front room of my cabin appeared warm and drowsy, as it had the night I almost died on Maray Point. As the coffee water boiled, I lifted my rocking chair and strode out the kitchen to the driveway. My battered 340 Duster sat next to Woody's field. Following the fresh tire tracks, I placed the chair on the driver's side and opened the door so the key in the ignition was visible. An impatient ambulance on Frazier Mountain Highway honked.

As I slumped into the rocker, my coffee mug from Yosemite slipped from my hand and suffered a rude introduction to the pavement. "Damn," I said. It was my only coffee cup. Lying on the ground, next to the broken glass, were a cotton ball and empty hypodermic.

Lingering beside my battered 340 Duster, Julie Christie combed the left side of my hair with her moist fingers. When I brushed her knuckles with my thumb, she scampered across Woody's field and slipped into the green glass of Valley Hospital.
Her presence in Lake of the Woods was so incredible I lost my equilibrium and the wheelchair slid into the 340 Duster.

At last I felt the morphine. Swells of warm narcotic caved in my left hip and flooded my genitals. In the southeast, the crater summit of Blue Mountain was encircled by a perfect ring of light from the shrouded moon.

TWENTY
Mt. Pinos

To this day no one knows what happened to Joaquin Murrieta's head.

On the porch, a rambunctious wind toyed with the screen door and banged it shut. 3 a.m. Focusing on my bedroom wall, I suffered a jolt. For an instant, in the faint glow of my orange night clock, I glimpsed the cop who shot himself sleeping in his hospital bed

My finger promptly tapped the buzzer.

"Good morning, Mr. Wiseass," a sweet voice chirped over the intercom.

I said, "How'd you know it was me?"

"Memo warns us about 3 a.m."

"I'm better now."

"Lucky you. Night shift is dullsville."

"Don't feel like the Lone Ranger."

She said, "I'll stop by to empty your urine bottle."

"I may not be good company."

"Not according to Nurse Christie."

I said, "I don't recognize your voice. Is this your first night of the week?

"Friday is my only night. I'm a candy striper."

Oh, perfect, a teenager.

Flinging off the army blanket, I raced to my desk in the writing room. In the bottom drawer was my petrified rock from Organ Pipe National Monument along with the remains of Dunham's Halloween package. Orange porch light was still shining. Stomping on the wooden steps, I started to reach back and turn it off, but decided to let it burn.

As I backed the battered 340 Duster onto Frazier Mountain Highway, there was absolutely no pain from my left hip or any other wound from Hughes Supermarket. Perhaps the crabby cashier had been correct about my recovery.

It was a lonely but familiar cruise into Lake of the Woods. Just beyond the historic welcome sign, constructed circa 1880, was Hampton's Village Market. Next door were the Mountain Coffee Shop, Cedar Ridge Tavern, and 76 Union service station. Across the street were a hardware store, gift shop, ranger station, post office, and May West Realty.

At the Cuddy Ski and Toboggan Rental Shop, I steered north on Cuddy Valley Road. Across the valley, with its blurred ranch lights, the hulking figure of Mt. Pinos emerged with a long wall of Jeffrey pine visible on its crooked ridge.

Sliding down the window, I stuck out my head and sucked the dry air that churned into Cuddy Valley from the Pacific. Between my legs was a cup of strong instant mud in a wine glass. Its steam tickled my nose. Wiping the moisture with a finger, I remembered the gobs of blood that had poured from my nose at Hughes Supermarket, and vetoed an examination.

My trip to Mt. Pinos ended so abruptly it seemed I had merely thought of the peak and was suddenly parked at its base. I nodded at the mountain. "Hey, gloomy guy."

As sunrise highballed into southern California, I approached the legendary Three-Finger Jack Trailhead, territory of mid-19th century Mexican bandits. The Three-Finger Jack Trail led to a primitive campsite named after Joaquin Murrieta, the most famous local *bandido*. One hundred and thirty years ago, the trail and camp had been used by the notorious outlaw following his guerrilla raids on American mining camps. During that time, with the exception of the monks from the Mission de San Fernando, few dared to enter the Tehachapi's. It is legendary that Mexican bandits always respected the cross.

Hiking Three-Finger Jack, I dwelled on my pain, or lack of it, and the accident. Very suspicious. Roaming the halls after 3 a.m., minus my body of course, I had read my medical charts in Dr. Kildare's office. Kidneys were bruised beyond recognition and blood saturated the urine and stool. Spleen and section of intestine had been removed and four ribs were snapped, piercing both lungs. 365 stitches. Internal bleeding, profuse and critical. Prognosis negative.

With stiff apprehension, I lifted my left pant leg and pushed down the wool sock. Just above the anklebone was a gruesome Frankenstein scar with fat, juicy suture marks.

At the primitive Joaquin Murrieta campsite, I dumped my pack in the dirt and leaned against a Jeffrey pine. Chewing a piece of cold bacon and drinking hot mud, I imagined Mexican *bandidos* and their *mujeres* moving about the camp. A rock fire pit, with an enormous pile of ash, was clear proof of J.'s recent backpack trip.

In a crouch, I sifted through the ash, and a puff of smoke slipped into the air. Fresh burnt pine. J. had not been the most recent visitor. Then, I saw it.

A queen of hearts was stuck between the bars of the iron grill. Words in what looked to be Dr. Kildare's handwriting read, "Garrett Kay, June 21,1947—November 8, 1974".

My nerves electrified. Inching backwards, methodically, I scanned the campsite perimeter. Someone was watching. Stumbling over my pack, I felt cold metal against the back of my thighs and plopped onto a hospital bed. It was so astonishing I didn't even attempt to move. The cop who shot himself was in the next bed reading my copy of Henry Miller's *Plexus*.

Dr. Kildare strolled into camp and scribbled something on my chart. "Kidney surgery in an hour," he said. "Time to play the game, Kay."

"What are my chances?"

"Decent, if you're angry enough."

Bolting out of bed, I stormed into a Jeffrey pine and bounced to the tile floor. The giant tree faded. In its place was a shattered ice cream freezer door at Hughes Supermarket on Balboa and Devonshire. Temperature on the porch post had dipped to nine degrees. My finger promptly tapped the buzzer.

"Wh-aat?" answered the nurse.

"Who is fucking with the temperature?"

"Such language! Who is this? The cop or wiseass?"

"Wiseass, I guess. I apologize, ma'am."

"Let me speak to the cop."

"He's reading Henry Miller."

"It's not time for your morphine shot, Mr. Kay."

A condor, huge as a boxcar, soared in a salty breath that blew up from the Pacific. It passed so near, riding the current of extinction, I could see its orange head and crooked white V underneath each wing. As it sailed behind a ridge, I found myself staring across Cuddy Valley at Blue Mountain. The burnt scar on its north summit resembled a silver necklace. A trail, with particular flair, slalomed down Butterscotch Creek with unnerving cutbacks. I stored a mental note.

"That trail has testicles."

Gold and Mexican monks invaded my thoughts. In the early 1800's, scores of monks had mined an obscure vein on Blue Mountain. During the Forty-Niner gold rush, the monks apparently sealed the entrance and camouflaged their trail because the location of their mine is still unknown. Records at the Mission de San Fernando were also destroyed.

There is a rumor, however, that the mine is situated on a northwestern slope near Blue Mountain's burnt scar. The rumor was given credence by the tale of an old rancher named Mr. Cuddy. It seems Mr. Cuddy was rounding up strays during the first blizzard of 1947 when he was thrown from his camel, a descendant of the Fort Tejon experiment, and tumbled on top of an iron door. In June, Mr. Cuddy returned but found nothing. He did leave a clue. He claimed the iron door was near 8,000 feet, because Lake Buena Vista was visible from the spot. This was an excellent clue in 1947 because Mt. Pinos blocked most of Lake Buena Vista from Blue Mountain. Unfortunately, today Lake Buena Vista is an oil field.

TWENTY-ONE
The Hiking Boots

It's wise not to piss in the bathtub.

Stomping my L.L. Bean hiking boots on the wooden step, I jiggled the key until there was a loud click. "No need to lock my door in Lake of the Woods," I said, tossing the key on the roof.

Cold front had lifted. Basking in the soft glow of the orange porch light, I checked the temperature on the porch post—forty-seven degrees.

In the field, giant snowflakes tumbled in slow motion, licking Woody's concrete marker. When I leaned over the porch railing, flakes stuck to my hair and eyelashes.

My refrigerator was mysteriously stocked with my favorite grub. Stacks of Delmonicos, crab, lettuce hearts, and jalapeño peppercorn dressing filled the shelves. There were Spanish olives, cheese, butter, bacon, OJ, bananas, and magnums of chardonnay. Cupboards were bulging with tuna, mayonnaise, yellow rice, raisins, cashews, sourdough bread, pancake batter, popcorn, and chocolate bars. Coffee, honey, and cans of Carnation evaporated milk were in the spice corner.

Ravenously, I devoured an enormous meal while saturating my veins with chardonnay. Parked on the couch, I listened to the potbelly stove purr with a cozy flame. It was time to drift, minus my body. In the next moment, I caromed off the beamed ceiling and executed a few cartwheels. On the couch, my intoxicated face grinned foolishly while lapping chardonnay.

A twig snapped on the ground outside. A prowler stalked the perimeter of my cabin. Footsteps, slow and deliberate, crunched past the side door and halted at my large picture window. Immediately I flew behind the TV. Captain James T. Kirk of the starship *Enterprise* had just punched an alien in what may have been...a nose?

Prowler remained stationary, scrutinizing G. Kay with his chardonnay. From behind the TV, I could only make out a silhouette. Continuing his probe, he circled the cabin to the wooden porch. I remembered the door was unlocked. Kitchen door creaked and my orange porch light was extinguished.

From Frazier Mountain Highway came the sound of whistling. It was the theme from *Lawrence of Arabia*. At least the prowler had taste. Springing from the TV, I turned the orange porch light back on with a swat. Scurrying down the center of Frazier Mountain Highway was a familiar figure wearing a long gray overcoat. It was the very same spook from Organ Pipe National Monument.

I said, "Holy shit, it's the ranger." Just my misfortune to be stranded on Blue Mountain with a peeping Tom, or Peter O'Toole.

I awoke with an empty glass in my hand. It was 3 a.m. I was bleary with chardonnay. On an impulse, I stumbled into the bathroom and knelt beside the tub. Plugging the drain, I let the water spill over my hand until it turned warm. As a precaution, I pressed my nose against the bathroom window and checked the perimeter in case the peeping Tom planned an encore.

For a long delicious moment, steaming water crept up my torso and soaked away the stress of Mt. Pinos. My testicles expanded luxuriously. In submersion, I spotted Julie Christie tiptoeing into the bathroom with a hypodermic in her moist hand. In usual fashion, I flew behind the TV. Channel 9 had an episode of *You Bet Your Life* with Groucho Marx. "Say the secret word," said Groucho, "the duck flies down and you win a hundred dollars."

A powerful piss was building in my bladder. My lungs were screaming. Good Lord, I forgot I was underwater. Bopping to the surface, I gasped for air and pissed into my plastic bottle.

The cop who shot himself said, "Something wrong?"

"The location of my urine is a mystery."

"Did you piss in your bath water?"

"Fuck, maybe."

"Does your piss still have blood?"

"I'll let you know when I find it."

He said, "Hey, Kay. While you were asleep a candy striper emptied your piss bottle. I think she took it."

"Was she a mink?"

"Real nice, but a youngster."

I said, "How's Henry Miller?"

"Glorious and disreputable."

Dripping on the cold tile floor, I clicked on the bathroom light and peeked into the tub. Water was crystal clear. Toilet water was also drinkable. Then I noticed the soggy floor. Damn! I still had on my L.L. Bean hiking boots.

TWENTY-TWO
The Morning After

There was a stalker in Lake of the Woods.

On the morning after, I kicked the army blanket off my bed and it flopped over the head of the cop who shot himself. Limping to the potbelly stove, I gathered some crumpled papers and chunks of pine. My legs felt one hundred years old.

"Is it over?" the cop who shot himself said.

"She took my morning samples an hour ago."

"Then why am I hiding?"

I said, "Hey, hero. Give me back my blanket."

"Who's fucking with the temperature?"

"I'm building a fire."

"Buzz the nurses, Kay."

"Not me. Nurses are weary of my shenanigans."

In the kitchen, I placed a tin of butter next to a gas flame and mixed enough batter to feed the entire wing. The smell of frying bacon filled the air. Orange porch light was still burning.

"I know you're listening," the cop who shot himself said into the intercom. "I hear you breathing. Who's messing with the temperature?"

"Who is this? The cop or wiseass?"

"Cop.

The nurse said cheerfully, "Good morning, officer. Maintenance will be there in a jiffy."

"Must be my rep with a firearm."

While my food cooked, I strolled into the living room and watched NBC. Barbara Walters was making a hullabaloo over an Indian summer in Manhattan.

On the porch, the Tehachapi sky was murky and in a foul mood. It had all the makings for a dismal day in Cuddy Valley. In front of my cabin I peered down both stretches of Frazier Mountain Highway. No signs of life. Buttoning up my leather coat, I decided it was time to hoof into town.

In the muddy streets of Lake of the Woods, I walked with the swagger of Steve McQueen in *Wanted: Dead or Alive.* Peeping Tom might bring a hefty reward.

At the first bend in Frazier Mountain Highway, a neon sign distracted my bounty hunting. It was Hampton's Village Market open for business. Loitering in the frigid street, I pictured Mrs. Hampton at the counter sipping a can of Buffalo beer.

The cop said, "What kind of beer?"

"Old lady Hampton loves Buffalo beer."

"Never heard of it."

"Local brew."

It was slightly disturbing to stand inside the empty market. A Kern County sheriff might figure I was robbing the place, if a Kern County sheriff happened to be on duty. Getting arrested could be the highlight of my day.

Next to the checkout stand was a little coffee maker with its red light on. A full pot of coffee sat on the burner. I said, "Mud." As I filled my cup, my eyes latched onto the parking lot in case a Seville from Balboa and Devonshire decided to swerve to avoid an empty shopping cart.

On the wall was a chart that read Sign For Goods and had a place for name and items. Feeling ridiculous, I signed, G. Kay—Coffee.

I waded into the muddy street. It began to snow. Normally it would only sleet in such intense cold, but the temperature on the porch post had returned to forty-seven degrees.

The cop who shot himself said, "Let me handle the nurses, Kay."

"Okay, but..."

"Yeah, yeah. The red-haired sweetie is all yours."

There was a frightful thud. I checked the perimeter and discovered the cop who shot himself had dropped his bedpan.

He said, "Better light a match."

The ranger station, May West Realty, and Cuddy Ski and Toboggan Rental Shop were closed, but the Cedar Ridge Tavern had its Olympia sign blinking. Not much action in the tavern. I stood over a rusty jukebox and scanned the selections. "No Dylan?" I put a quarter in the slot and punched G4.

As I leaned over the wooden bar and put a head on an Olympia draft, Kenny Rogers started singing "Just Dropped In To See What Condition My Condition Was In." I flopped into a booth next to the pool table. Someone had been playing a game, but left without finishing. The twelve and fifteen balls were spotted and the cue ball was cushioned near a side pocket. The eight ball was set up for a tight bank. It was my choice to take the quackers and attempt a better set-up on the eight, or gamble on the bank. I noticed a glass of beer sitting on the corner of the table. I walked over to the edge and took a taste. It was cold and still fresh. Whoever had been drinking had just left.

I said, "I think I almost collected a bounty." Peeping Tom must have been playing a solitary game of pool, but bolted out the back door when he heard the cop's bedpan.

I said, "Unsociable bastard. Doesn't want to have a beer with me or play pool."

Plucking a pool stick, I rattled the table and banked the eight ball into a corner pocket. On the chart, I signed, G. Kay—Two Olympia Draft and Pool.

"My treat, chickenshit," I yelled at the back door.

TWENTY-THREE
Lake Buena Vista

Mr. Cuddy is no ordinary man.

The cop who shot himself said, "It's got me miffed, Kay. Who calls the mountain Blue?"

"I told you, locals." I paused under the orange porch light and stomped my L.L. Bean hiking boots on the wooden steps. "Damn, nine degrees."

"My parents spend a week in those mountains every Christmas and they call it…"

"The name on the map."

"Why can't I say the other name?"

"It prefers to be called Blue."

"Who prefers?"

"It's the password, okay? If you use the password, Lake of the Woods will welcome you aboard."

"What about the name on the map?"

I said, "It's not the password. Blue Mountain is the password."

Slipping down the upper section of Iris Ridge, I delighted in scuffing the fresh powder with my L.L. Bean hiking boots. Squeak squeak. "God, this is fun." Squeak squeak.

In the center of a small clearing were two hospital beds with a pair of overhead lamps. The cop who shot himself and I were watching the A.M. Movie on KTTV. Jack Palance had just gunned down a little shitkicker in a muddy Wyoming street. Lurking near the foot of my bed stood a shadowy figure. As I inched closer to the scene, the figure dodged behind the great southern oak, which appeared to have strayed from its home on Maray Point.

"I swear that tree has moved."

The cop said, "Jack Palance is a menace."

"He's scary. I also think he's hiding behind the great southern oak."

"Jack Palance? Why do you say that?"

"It's either him or his twin brother."

"Check it out, Kay."

I walked toward the oak. "Hey, mister. I saw you duck behind the tree. Come on out."

A rugged elderly gentleman, with a long gray overcoat and the malicious twinkle of Jack Palance, appeared beside the great southern oak and blocked my path. "*Buenos dias*," he said with a grin. He reached out to shake my hand, but I kept my distance as if we were sparring in a boxing ring.

The cop said, "It's just an old man."

"No ordinary old man."

The old man said, "You appear to have seen a ghost."

"You startled me."

"Friends claim I have a nasty habit of spooking people on Blue Mountain. My apologies, please."

"I'm over it," I said, returning his smile.

"It's good to see you smile, Garrett. A man shouldn't be too serious."

"How do you know my name?"

"I know all the names in Lake of the Woods."

"We've met before, haven't we? You're very familiar."

"Perhaps."

The long gray overcoat was vintage bandit apparel. "Perhaps in the desert or hospital?"

"I enjoy the desert in the fall."

"I was just released from Valley Hospital on Van Nuys and Sherman Way."

"Nothing serious, I hope."

"If you know all the names in Lake of the Woods you should be well aware of my accident at Hughes Supermarket in Granada Hills. It was on TV."

"I don't own a TV."

I said, "You were also a patient at Valley Hospital. We were roommates for an evening. Didn't talk, though."

He nodded. "I'm surprised you recognized me. Naturally, I was warned. 'Wiseass,' they said."

"Who said?"

"My sources."

"What sources?"

"It wouldn't be right to name names. Let me explain." He leaned against the great southern oak. I was positive that tree was not in its right spot. "Years ago I fell off my camel and tore a knee ligament. Damn thing never healed properly. This year, on the twenty-seventh anniversary, I stumbled while chasing a runaway shopping cart. If it wasn't for bad luck—."

"I'd have no luck at all."

He grinned. "I'm recovered now. Dr. Kildare said I only needed fresh air and exercise."

"Dr. Kildare?"

"Pretty red-haired nurse, too."

His story was fascinating. A camel and a shopping cart. My defenses were lowered. I decided not to dwell on the night I saw him at Valley Hospital, or in the desert. Not yet, anyhow. Comradery seemed to gush from his grizzled face. My blood felt warm and alive and I believed he was responsible.

He looked at me for a long moment. "How many days did you spend at Valley Hospital?"

I was plunged into uncertainty. With a simple question he had bullied me into a corner. I glanced at the cop who shot himself. This was no ordinary old man. I said, "Too many."

"I'm glad you've also recovered. You were magnificent coming down Iris Ridge. For a moment I thought you were a mule deer." Apparently this was a compliment from an old mountain man.

"Thank you."

"Was something chasing you?"

"No, I was mountain slipping."

He nodded as if my answer made perfect sense. "It looked like someone was chasing you."

I laughed. "I certainly don't know who that would be. Until this moment, I thought I was the only person in Lake of the Woods. Where is everyone?"

"They'll be back."

"Why did they leave?"

He scratched his chin. "It's cold."

"Cold?"

"You don't understand. Lake of the Woods is populated with elderly ranchers and retired miners. Severe cold may not hamper your style, but the elderly don't function in such extremes."

"It's only a front."

"No, it's different. It's nine degrees, quite uncharacteristic in the Tehachapi's. You can check every cavalry record from Fort Tejon or monk ledger at Mission de San Fernando. Average November temperature in Lake of the Woods is forty-seven degrees."

"What about the permanent residents and businesses?"

"They'll be back."

"You and I are alone?"

"We're not totally abandoned. Most businesses are still open. There's no one to collect money. Just sign your name and debt on the charts and square up in the spring."

"It's still disturbing."

"No need to brood."

I tilted my head. "Who told you about me?"

"My sources."

"No fair. Who told?"

"A nurse or two," he said, "and the cop who shot himself."

"You *know* the cop who shot himself?"

"The cop warned me, 'Kay is moody, but a good sport. All mangled up and still a wiseass.' "

"He has little room to talk."

"Beat me twice in Monopoly."

"Don't feel like the Lone Ranger."

"I've scheduled a rematch."

I said, "If the elderly don't function well in the cold, what are you doing here?"

"I beg your pardon."

"No disrespect, but you're elderly."

"I only appear elderly."

"It's been sunup for only three minutes and we are two miles and three thousand feet from Lake of the Woods. There are no roads. If you took the Pacific Crest it's six miles. How did you get up here so quickly?"

"Might ask you the same question."

I pointed. "My bed is in that clearing."

He nodded. "My mornings begin at 3 a.m. Never lived anywhere else but in the Tehachapi's. I know these parts better than anyone. I'm seventy-seven, but in good physical shape. Perhaps I'm as tough as you."

I checked his Jack Palance physique. "No doubt."

"Besides, my name is Mr. Cuddy. Surely you've heard of me. My folks were the
first U.S. citizens to settle the valley."

"What valley?"

"Don't you know the valley between Pinos and Blue Mountain is named Cuddy?"

"Yeah. Wow, I missed the connection."

"Maybe you've heard of Cuddy Creek, Cuddy Road, Cuddy Bald, or Cuddy Ski and Toboggan Rentals?"

I felt foolish. "No need to rub it in."

"I'm the last of the Cuddy's."

I said, "Hold on a minute. You mentioned a camel. Are you the Mr. Cuddy who discovered the monks' gold mine in 1947?"

He smiled, proudly. "In the flesh."

"I heard you died in the early '60's."

"My beloved camel died November 8, 1964."

I said, "This is an incredible honor. Sorry about your camel."

His handshake was firm. This old man was a celebrity in the Tehachapi's. Legendary. His family had tamed Cuddy Valley before the Mexican-American War and had marched into L.A. with Kit Carson and John C. Fremont. In the 1880's, the Cuddy's founded Lake of the Woods and purchased the last camels from the U.S. Army at Fort Tejon for cattle roundups. Mr. Cuddy was notorious for roaming Blue Mountain on his favorite camel, with a double-barreled shotgun tucked underneath his long gray overcoat. Mrs. Hampton once bragged of the day in the late '50's she spotted Mr. Cuddy aboard his camel galumphing above Maray Point.

"Did he have his shotgun?" I asked her.

"Hell, yeah, he had his shotgun," she said, sipping on a can of Buffalo beer. "Old bastard used it to wave at me."

"What do you know about the gold mine on Blue Mountain?" Mr. Cuddy asked me.

"If you're referring to the monks' treasure, I think it's a fairy tale."

"Really? Are you familiar with the stories of the bandit on Blue Mountain?"

"Which bandit?"

"Murrieta, of course. Joaquin Murrieta. My great-grandfather sold Murrieta cattle and tequila. They got along famously."

"What does Murrieta have to do with the monks?"

"Murrieta hid his gold inside the monks' mine. Not even the U.S. Army would mess with the Catholic Church. Of course, the monks would never bother with bandit loot."

"What kept the bandits from bothering with monks' loot?"

"Respect for the cross."

"Another fairy tale."

"Oh, no," he said, solemnly. "Murrieta considered himself a defender of Mexico and the cross. But you are familiar with the old stories, eh?"

"Of course."

"And you know of my experiences with the monks' mine?"

"I've read about it in books. 1947 was the year I was born."

"Interesting. What have you read?"

I said, "Actually, it's quite a mystery. You claimed to have discovered the mine during the winter of '47, but couldn't relocate it the next summer.

"Not quite. I did discover the entrance to the mine in January of 1947."

"Now you can't find it?"

"Still playing hide and go seek with me."

"What exactly happened in '47?"

He said, "Books are mostly accurate. A large Jeffrey crashed in the woods and spooked my camel, tossing me over Butterscotch Creek. My leg smashed onto an iron door sticking out of the snow. Here's my bum knee to prove it. I'm certain it was the entrance to the old mine. Double treasure, monks' gold and bandit loot. A blizzard chased me off Blue Mountain that day, but I wasn't concerned. I know this country better than anyone and my markings were true. Elevation was about eight thousand feet. It was obvious because I was level with the summit of Cuddy Bald. Most incredible, however, was the sight of Lake Buena Vista balancing perfectly on the pointy-head of Mt. Pinos twenty-seven miles away.

"Christ."

"But when I returned in late June, I couldn't find my position, because Lake Buena Vista had strangely become…"

"Dry," I blurted.

"Dried up June 21, 1947."

"Impossible."

"Bone dry. Southern California lakes are notorious for draining into earthquake faults."

"But how could…?"

He held up his hand. "I've taken too much of your time. You seemed to be in such a hurry."

"I'd like to walk with you if you're going down."

"I'm going up. Still combing for that iron door. But we'll talk again. Be certain of it."

I said, "One question." Mr. Cuddy stopped but did not turn around. "Still carrying that shotgun?"

He opened the long gray overcoat that hung past his knees, and slid out a vintage double-barreled shotgun. Bracing the butt against his thigh, he pointed at the sky. KABLAM KABLAM. The echoes ripped up Blue Mountain and exploded over the crater summit.

"To my camel," Mr. Cuddy said.

TWENTY-FOUR
Morphine

A friend with dope is a friend with hope.

"Answer me," I barked into the intercom. "I hear you breathing.

The cop said, "She's fed up."

"It's her job."

"May I help you?" the nurse finally replied, icily.

"Is it time for my pain medication?"

"Who is this? The cop or wiseass?"

"Wiseass, I guess."

"Your next shot is scheduled in two hours."

"May we reschedule?"

"Describe your pain, please."

I said, "Like broken glass in my veins."

"One moment." For luck I zipped to my place behind the TV. "One of these days, Alice," Jackie Gleason bellowed, "to the moooooon!"

"Nice metaphor," the cop who shot himself said.

The nurse announced, "Dr. Kildare has authorized a shot."

"Thank you, ma'am."

"You're not fooling any of the nurses, Mr. Kay."

"My gosh," Julie Christie said, entering the room. "You're turning blue."

"Holding my breath."

"Stop it."

"I was waiting for you."

"Only because I bring the shot."

"Not true, Mrs. Miller. It's much more."

When she pulled up my hospital gown, I was swamped with desire for the green Girl Scout sleeping bag. Her uniform fit snugly over her pleasing butt. Smearing alcohol over my hip with a cotton ball, she removed the cover on the needle with her teeth and pinched a layer of skin. My index finger rubbed her knuckle.

Julie Christie said, "There are guys staying at Valley Hospital who fall in love with me."

"So?"

"You're not one of them, are you?"

"What if I am?"

"Don't be fooled. It's not me you want."

"It's not?"

"It's only the security of the uniform and the shot."

"I think it's partially what's under the uniform."

"You're wrong, Garrett."

"After I recover, would you consider testing your theory?" I challenged.

An odd expression appeared on her face. "I might. Promise me you'll recover?"

"Sure. Why wouldn't I recover? What a goofy promise."

When Julie Christie was in the hallway, the cop who shot himself lifted up his sheets and displayed over twenty vials of morphine.

He said, "Hurry up, Loco Loco, take it. I'm a fucking cop."

"For me?"

"It's pay back."

"What pay back?"

"For my combat training."

Fitting a vial into the hypodermic, I pulled down my Levi's and poured chardonnay over my hip. Lacking the grace of Julie Christie, I fumbled a bit and then bopped morphine into my butt. The cop who shot himself gathered up the paraphernalia and dumped it into the potbelly stove.

He said, "Jesus, now I'm a fucking accomplice."

There was a brief squabble on the floor over the missing morphine, but no one suspected the two twenty-seven-year-olds in room 9 who were so fucked up.

TWENTY-FIVE
Butterscotch Creek

No one gets a head start.

Ducking under my army blanket, I inhaled a whiff of butterscotch spiced with kelp and Pacific spray. The cop who shot himself had fallen asleep while watching TV.

I said, "Poor bastard. Out cold on half a pill."

"No, I'm not," he said loudly.

"Jesus, you scared me. What are you doing?"

"Pretending to sleep."

"What for?"

"I know better, Loco Loco. You won't travel if you think I'm awake."

"So that's how you keep tagging along."

"Why did you stop hiking?"

"I'm inspecting a dead Jeffrey pine."

As I poked my nose into the Jeffrey's bark and cobwebs, the delicious aroma of butterscotch filled the air. Though the pine had been dead for years, its scent still lingered in the wood.

Within sight of the 27 giant Jeffreys, a numbing sensation washed over my feet and chilled my ankles. I had inadvertently waded into Butterscotch Creek. Though the bed was bone dry, I felt a curious surge of melting snow.

I said, "It's a trick, only a trick."

As I sloshed to the middle, the sensation crept up to my shrinking balls. With a cupped hand I scooped an imaginary drink. Even with no water I still choked.

"May I help you?" a nurse said over the intercom.

The cop said, "Kay doesn't look too sharp."

"Who?"

"The wiseass."

"What's the problem?"

"He's choking."

She checked the charts. "Did he drink water?"

"I'm not sure. Why?"

"Wiseass always chokes on water."

Focusing on the legendary grove, I spotted a figure in a long gray overcoat scurrying down Iris Ridge. It was admirable the way Mr. Cuddy tucked that vintage shotgun under his coat. At Butterscotch Creek he plopped on all fours and tested the dried bed with his finger. Satisfied, he took a drink.

I shouted, "No water, Mr. Cuddy."

He glanced in my direction; it was obvious he saw me, but he didn't nod or grin. When he raised his fist, a crosswind cut across the treetops with the ferocity of a jet fighter. My concentration disintegrated. Butterscotch Creek gushed to its banks with rushing water.

"It's only a trick," I repeated. "Fucking trick."

The cop said, "What's the matter, Kay? Snap out of it."

The freezing water caused my legs to turn to mush. I called out, "Mr. Cuddy, it's me, Garret Kay. Don't run off." Flares from his double-barreled shotgun lit up the sky. It was a clear challenge to race.

The cop said, "Catch him, Kay."

122

The old man infuriated me. "I don't want to play his stupid game."

Splashing across icy Butterscotch Creek, I crashed into brittle woods and hammered the dead branches with my fists. Each whack sounded like a sharp report from a pistol. Mr. Cuddy appeared on my left flank, rapidly losing ground.

"Nice surge, Kay," the cop who shot himself said.

"Wait until I put on my spikes."

At Maray Point I unleashed a fierce attack, weaving and caroming off the slope. Reaching the paved road, I ignited a roaring kick and didn't stop until I had slapped the porch railing. Orange porch light was off. When I touched the bulb it was still hot. Reaching inside, I flicked the switch and the bulb popped to life.

"Now what?" the nurse said over the intercom.

I said, "My mistake."

"Who is this? The cop or wiseass?"

"Take a chance."

Puke leaped out my nostrils. My lungs were raspy and on fire. Glancing down Frazier Mountain Highway, I spotted Mr. Cuddy strutting with obvious merriment towards Lake of the Woods. My chin hit the porch railing.

"Old dude beat me down Iris Ridge," I gasped.

"You blundered, Kay."

"How so?"

"No one gets a head start."

TWENTY-SIX
Mission De San Fernando

The cop who shot himself knows Mr. Cuddy.

Once again the cop who shot himself appeared in the small meadow on his hospital bed. He freshened my glass of chardonnay and put away his Monopoly board.

He said, "You play like shit."

"I'm not a businessman."

"Do you really like this wine, Kay? Don't humor me."

"It's my favorite."

"Perhaps we like the same wine because we're both in critical condition."

"Injured on the same morning."

"Same age."

I said, "Seville and Smith and Wesson."

He smiled. "I just wanted to put my pants on. Didn't mean to fuck up the widow's Labrador."

"Don't talk about it."

"No, it's important. I was unfair. You were all mangled up and I made jokes about your bloody piss."

"One day we'll both laugh about my bloody piss."

"Let me show you my next dump. You need to see the red mush in my bedpan."

I said, "Oh, don't bother."

"No, I insist. You deserve to see because I fucked with you. But you never spooked. All mangled up and you're still a wiseass."

"I'm a huge coward."

"Kildare has recommended medals."

"He was being sarcastic."

"Until you came along, I only shit blood and waited for the trucks on Sherman Way. But you changed my attitude. Quit is no longer in my vocabulary."

"I had little to do with it."

"You're my best friend."

"What about the trucks?"

"Trucks made a monkey out of me, Kay."

"How so?"

"I listened every night at 3 a.m. because I thought they were going places. But the trucks have been only going in circles. You and I are going places."

On a whim, I removed my silver bracelet from Blue Mountain and thrust it into the light. Engraved on the inside was *Mission de San Fernando.* There was no longer any doubt. Mr. Cuddy had rediscovered the fabled mine in June of '47. But what was his game? How could he be certain I would find the silver bracelet?

I said, "Why didn't you tell me you had met Mr. Cuddy?"

"At first I didn't recognize him. He appeared at my worst moment."

"But you knew it was him."

"Not really. In the hospital he seemed different. He wasn't nearly as frightening."

"Wonder how he rigged his shotgun to shoot flares?"

TWENTY-SEVEN
Fire of '47

It was time to play a trick on Mr. Cuddy.

Sometimes the creek had water; other times it was dry. I stored a mental note. Butterscotch Creek was dry when I concentrated, but had water if I suffered a lapse.

The cop said, "Man, you stink. Have you been smoking?"

"I'm standing in the burnt-out area."

"What's that?"

"Section of Blue Mountain that was burned in the great fire of '47. June, I think."

"How badly was it burned?"

"Only a slim section near the summit was touched. The great fire raged across half of the Los Padres but only nicked Blue Mountain on the throat." From Mt. Pinos the burnt-out area looked like a silver necklace.

"Did any trees survive?"

"Only dusty bush." I scouted the area. "Hold it, there's a lone Jeffrey pine stuck in its heart."

"Check it out."

On my way to the Jeffrey, I stumbled in the dirt and lost my hiking boot. "Goddamn it."

"What happened?"

"Burnt-out area gave me a flat."

I reached into the bush and discovered a raggedy strip of rubber next to my L.L. Bean hiking boot. It could have been from an old tire. I stood next to the solitary pine and whacked the strip against its trunk.

An army of bulldozers cranked their engines and proceeded to topple trees and chew up the north slope. I blinked my eyes and looked at the cop who shot himself. "Did you change the channel?"

"No, I didn't." His remote control sat harmlessly on the night table. "What is it?"

I said, "I see the fire coming."

"You see what?"

"I see the fire of '47 coming from Fort Tejon."

"Bullshit, Kay. Blue Mountain burned twenty-seven years ago."

"She's going to burn today."

Squadrons of firefighters manned chainsaws while others dug trenches or set grass and kindling on fire.

I said, "It's hopeless. This fire is taking no prisoners."

"Fire crews must have been successful. You said yourself only a slim section got tagged."

"I see Mr. Cuddy. He's riding his camel."

"His what?"

"I see it, but don't believe it."

The cop said, "Tell me."

"Mr. Cuddy is rounding up the fire.

"What are you talking about?"

I said, "You know, like a cowboy with his cattle. Mr. Cuddy is blasting his shotgun and rounding up the fire."

"Don't fuck with me, Kay."

"I'm not. The fire is stampeding south."

The great fire of '47, igniting at Fort Tejon and leaping the Grapevine, had swept south of Blue

Mountain and never licked its slopes. Mr. Cuddy never received any credit. Volunteers had loaded their equipment and rushed south to dig another firebase on Gormon plateau.

I said, "It just occurred to me that if the fire of '47 happened in June, there was no burnt-out area when Mr. Cuddy got tossed by his camel."

"So?"

"That's why he did it. He rounded up the fire to keep the monks' mine a secret."

Snatching the piece of bulldozer tire, I flung it across the burnt-out area and Mr. Cuddy popped up where it landed. I ducked under the red manzanita, but he didn't seem to take notice. With the old weathered strip in his wrinkled paw, Mr. Cuddy remained fixed to his spot. I watched him run his fingertips along the rubber's edge and scan the upper section of Blue Mountain with a preternatural radar that crackled in the scrub.

"Old bastard isn't human."

The cop warned, "Do not change your position."

When Mr. Cuddy clawed the tire, it felt as though his fingernails skinned my spine. Then he licked the tread. Jumping to my feet, I wiped a sticky honey off the nape of my neck. I raised my fist, but he didn't acknowledge my salute. Instead he dashed into the forest and disappeared.

At the 27 giant Jeffreys, I looked around the supermarket and broke my concentration. Instantly, Butterscotch Creek exploded with bold, rollicking water. For an experiment, I picked up a sturdy log and pitched it into the current. I poured on the juice and attempted to run on its shoulder, but the current was too swift. I stored another mental note—Butterscotch Creek can outrun me.

Mr. Cuddy was waiting for me at the paved road, this time ambushing my wounded expression with a video camera. I snarled, "Turn it off."

"It's my job, Garrett," he said, innocently. He seemed amused by my temper. "I'm a contributing photographer for *National Geographic* and *Wild Kingdom*." I'd won a small measure of victory. This time I didn't puke.

Strutting like Jack Palance in the classic western *Shane*, Mr. Cuddy stepped forward with his fancy camera still clicking. It was absurd. When I finally broke out laughing, he lowered the camera and grinned.

"Sense of humor is essential."

I said, "Essential for what?"

"To counter the brooding."

"Why film me?"

"You're strong and graceful. I've observed you several times doing what you call mountain slipping, and your style is unique."

"I'm learning about you too."

He said, "It took me nearly a century to prepare for the Tehachapi's. You have natural talent."

"If I'm so talented, how did you beat me to the paved road?"

"I don't understand. I've been waiting here for an hour."

"You were at the burnt-out area thirty minutes ago."

"Not me."

"I saw you."

"People say I've wandered Blue Mountain so often that a part of me doesn't come down."

"Which part outran me to the paved road?"

He shook his head. "Is it so incomprehensible that old Mr. Cuddy could beat you down Blue Mountain? I know her slopes and terrain better than anyone."

I decided to make my best stand. "I don't doubt your trailblazing. You returned to Blue Mountain in the spring of '47 and rediscovered the monks' iron door."

He said, "No, it was June 21st, the day you were born."

My turn to gloat. For a moment Mr. Cuddy appeared confused. I held up my left arm with the silver bracelet and winked. Then he realized to what extent he had been duped.

"Nasty trick. Shame on you."

"It's obvious you never lost track of the mine."

"Why?"

"What was the name of your camel?"

He tilted his head. "Her name was Duster."

I thought of my own battered 340 Duster. "No way Duster would have forgotten the coordinates."

"Very few people know about the mine, and they're all dead."

"Not me."

"No, not you."

"I know something else. You and Duster rounded up the great fire of '47."

He grinned. "Didn't get much credit. Damn, you're good."

I said, "You're the one who is good. But you can't whip me down Blue Mountain." I was determined to show bravado. "Not because you're too old. You're incredible and I don't doubt your skill or endurance. But mountain slipping is *my* sport. Once I figure the route, you will not whip me down the mountain."

"I travel differently. Would it suffice to say I know a few shortcuts?"

"How did you know my birthday?"

"My sources."

"Not even the cop or Julie Christie knows my birthday."

"Other sources."

I said, "You owe me. I told you about the mine and great fire of '47."

"Harry Kay told me."

"Harry Kay? I don't understand."

"Harry Kay and I were friends for fifty years."

"*You* were friends with my grandfather?"

"Sure, good friends. Same age too."

"That's right, you're seventy-seven. You must have met Harry Kay when you were both twenty-seven."

"Same age as you, and most of your friends."

"When Harry Kay was twenty-seven, he spent two months in a hospital. He nearly died."

"We met in that hospital."

"It was in northern Minnesota."

Mr. Cuddy said, "On a fishing trip to Lake Vermillion, I cracked my knee in a boating accident. At the hospital, it was Harry Kay who helped me get over my depression."

"Why was Harry Kay in the hospital?"

"He suffered a gruesome steam-shovel accident in the Eveleth mine."

131

"Harry Kay never mentioned you to me."

"You've never mentioned any of your friends to me. Who are your friends?"

"Not many."

"What are their names?"

"I…"

"You owe me. I told you about Harry Kay."

I said, "Alright, let's see. There's Larson, Dunham, J., Julie Christie, and—." It felt peculiar naming my closest friends to Mr. Cuddy. I eyeballed him suspiciously.

"And?" Somehow he was manipulating me.

"And the cop who shot himself."

TWENTY-EIGHT
A Very Fine List

It's all a memory.

Lounging in my rocker with a healthy dose of chardonnay, I watched flames from the potbelly stove lick at an elusive draft whistling under the doorjamb.

My lonely existence had been reduced to living in a hamlet called Lake of the Woods, with a spooky old man as a companion. Events from October 31st to the present contained a lifetime.

It was time to formulate a list. Organ Pipe National Monument, Sierra del Ajo, Halloween 1974. Balboa and Devonshire, Hughes Supermarket, a dog vet, x-ray man chili beans, and Valley Hospital. Lake of the Woods, Joaquin Murrieta, 3:00 a.m., and the temperature on the porch post. Cocaine, morphine, chardonnay, and the cop who shot himself. Burgundy piss and red mush. Mountain slipping, double-barreled shotgun, J., Dunham, Ms. D., Dr. Kildare Julie Christie, and Harry Kay. 1947, 77, 27 giant Jeffreys. Butterscotch Creek, Iris Ridge, Maray Point, and the great southern oak. Orange porch light. Larson and a Seville. Shopping cart, Mt. Pinos, aisle 9, room 9, and Mr. Cuddy. Blue Mountain.

It was a very fine list. All these people, places and things were no longer mysterious or indecipherable. They were my memories.

TWENTY-NINE
Red Flag

Mail call in Lake of the Woods

At sunrise, I drifted toward Lake of the Woods in search of jellies and hot mud. Sky was smoked glass, not a cloud or soaring bird was out of place.

Trudging along Frazier Mountain Highway, I hunted for pinecones and booted them into the air with my L.L. Bean hiking boots.

I said, "God, this is a kick."

One cone tumbled next to an old shack. Another bounced off a two-story A-frame with four Jeffreys growing through its sundeck. People who lived in these homes were my neighbors, yet I couldn't recall a single face or personality. Familiar vibrations, however, danced in the air and crackled.

On the porch of Cimarron Gifts was a sign that read, We Are Open—Wade On In. The shop was cluttered and cozy. I tapped the service bell.

"Not even remotely close to breakfast, Mr. Wiseass," a nurse yawned over the intercom.

"How did you know I wasn't the cop?"

"He had surgery and is spending the night in recovery."

I looked in the clearing and his bed was indeed empty. "Any word?"

"Word?"

"On the cop."

"Yes, he's recovering."

On the shelves of Cimarron Gifts were post cards and place mats, painted dishes and carvings, nature sketches, glass figurines, an assortment of wind chimes, customized jewelry, local history and nature books, lamps, ceramics, macramé, stained glass, candles, and cuckoo clocks. Sitting on the edge of a counter was a blue Lake of the Woods coffee mug. In the past I had scorned such tacky items, but today I felt different. Near the front door was a sign-out sheet for purchases. Placing the mug inside my leather coat, I signed, G. Kay—Lake of the Woods mug.

In an alley behind Cimarron Gifts was the back lot of Cuddy Ski and Toboggan Rentals. Peeking through the chain-link fence, I focused on the various sleds and toboggans fitted snugly on their racks. It was tempting to rent a toboggan, but I wasn't up to wrestling with the barbwire fence. I stored another mental note.

It was warm and drowsy in Hampton's Village Market. Little red light shone on the coffee maker. Filling my new mug, I noticed a shopping cart with a Hughes Supermarket logo.

"What are you doing in Lake of the Woods?"

The cop said, "Shopping carts can't talk, Loco Loco."

"It's from Hughes."

"Bring it back to room nine."

I said, "How's your recovery?"

"I don't know. Kildare has a mean poker face."

On the trip home I made a startling discovery. Near a rundown wooden church the Hughes shopping cart rolled to the entrance of a rumpled cemetery and locked its wheels. For an instant I thought I spotted a shadow inside the church and it caused my heart to thump twice. The scene was eerie and familiar.

The cop said, "Stay clear of that place."

Using the shopping cart as cover, I drifted among the tombstones and glanced at the names. In a far corner of the cemetery was a fresh grave marked: H. Kay, April 3, 1897—November 8, 1974.

"Tried to warn you."

"It's only a trick." But I was visibly shaken, and stumbled. My new Lake of the Woods mug slipped from my coat and chipped its rim.

Leaning on Harry Kay's headstone was a shovel, a clear and compelling invitation to make things right. It was my chance to attend my grandfather's funeral.

The cop said, "Do not dig up that grave, Kay."

"It's something I've got to do."

Despite the twenty-seven degrees temperature, sweat dripped from my chin and splashed into the hole. Soon the shovel struck wood. Brushing back the damp earth, I lit a match. Leaning over for a closer examination, I discovered a small note taped to the top of the coffin.

"Fuck no," I shouted, tossing the shovel into the air.

Striking another match, I lowered my face into the grave and read the note.

Dear Garrett, thanks for attending my funeral. Sorry to disappoint, but gramps didn't put up much of a struggle. My performance was not very respectable.

Harry Kay
P.S. - Go back to the cemetery gate.

Resting on the coffin, I recalled the summer of 1954 in northern Minnesota. In an effort to show off my swimming prowess, I swam under the dock and apparently tried to take out a piling with my head. Harry Kay reached into Lake Vermillion and fished me out by my hair.

Harry Kay said, "What impressed me most was that you continued to struggle. Though you were drowning and nearly unconscious, you refused to let go without a good fight. I admire that in a man. You've taught your grandfather a fine lesson."

When Harry Kay had been struck by a steam shovel, he huddled in Ely Memorial and prepared for war. But Harry Kay was too strong and Mr. Cuddy could only rattle him in the same fashion he had rattled Larson on Sierra del Ajo.

At the entrance to the graveyard, within sight of the rundown wooden church, I saw what Harry Kay had planned for me. Red flag on the mailbox was up.

The cop who shot himself said, "Nothing I'd want to read."

"It's from my grandfather." Placing the red flag down, I gently opened the box. Inside was a small envelope.

Someone was eyeballing me. A quick scan of the perimeter revealed nothing suspicious or out of place. No shadows or parted curtains.

Only Blue Mountain.

THIRTY
Harry Kay's Letter

Crumpled papers, morphine, and a map.

> *Dear Garrett, I was certain you would come to Lake of the Woods. My old friend Mr. Cuddy is anxious about your arrival. Beware.*
>
> *I'm proud Blue Mountain hasn't intimidated you. She's always watching. I nicknamed her the peeping Tom.*
>
> *You're training for a race or game, and working out in the Tehachapi's with the same intensity of your senior cross country season. Granada Hills had a tenacious team in 1964.*
>
> *When I was twenty-seven, my situation was as precarious as your ridiculous accident. After my chest was crushed by a steam shovel, I huddled in Ely Memorial and prepared for war. Mr. Cuddy would only run a time trial.*
>
> *At seventy-seven Harry was weak and too filled with grief to race. Don't concern yourself with my grief. I never wanted to let go without a struggle. Remember the summer of '54 when you tried to take out my dock with your head? You even bitched when I pulled your hair. Only a little shit and already a wiseass. I stored a mental note. In my time trial with the steam shovel, I whipped Mr. Cuddy down Blue*

Mountain. Today I wasn't prepared for the grief.

Grief, I thought. What grief?

Forget about my grief. We have been good for each other. Though I am seventy-seven and you twenty-seven, we have always been at the same stage of the hoop.
Your Grandfather,
Harry Kay

I said, "Did your wife bring more chardonnay?"

"No, we're in for a grim evening."

"I'd piss blood for a glass of chardonnay."

"Is it really your favorite? You aren't just humoring me?

"In the cabin, the owl-shade lamp is shining on my desk in the writing room. It would be heaven to sit at my desk with a healthy glass of chardonnay."

The cop said, "Grab your piss bottle, Loco Loco. I lied. Just wanted to be certain you weren't fucking with me."

"You are demented."

"What do you keep on your desk?"

"Who cares?"

"It may reveal something."

"God, I hope not. Only see my crumpled papers and morphine."

P.S.- Go to the Lake of the Woods post office and open box 627. Key is taped to the back of the letter. In the box is a gift for the lesson you taught me in 1954. Read it at your writing desk with your crumpled papers and morphine.

Harry Kay had flipped. How did he know about my crumpled papers and morphine? As a precaution, I started to torch the letter.
"No," I said. "I want to add it to my papers."

THIRTY-ONE
Tunnels

It's a pain in the ass to run carrying a stopwatch.

Hopping off my wooden porch, I strode into Lake of the Woods with a purpose. Temperature on the porch post was a pleasant forty-seven degrees.

Cuddy Ski and Toboggan Rentals remained closed, but the shopping carts were lined neatly in front of Hampton's Village Market and the red Olympia neon was blinking at Cedar Ridge Tavern.

With so much mud and snow caked on the highway, the year could have been 1847. At any moment, Mexican *bandidos* led by Joaquin Murrieta might stampede through town. Next to May West realty, the post office was the only modern structure in town. The Stars and Bars appeared drunk on its pole.

In box 627 was a slip of paper. Harry Kay's key fit snugly, accompanied by a loud click. I leaned on a windowsill and read out loud to the cop who shot himself.

> *Dear Garrett, when I whipped Mr. Cuddy down Blue Mountain, I used a secret passage that runs from Butterscotch Creek to Iris Ridge. I code-named the passage Tunnels. It winds down Blue Mountain in a long smooth S. Fir and old growth piñón pine form thick walls and a ceiling. After I whipped Mr. Cuddy to the paved road, he's roamed the north slope for*

> *fifty years searching for Tunnels. His weary excuse of hunting for monks' gold is pure rubbish.   Harry Kay*
>
> *P.S. – In your workouts, use my old stopwatch.*

"Didn't Harry Kay tell you to read the letter at home with your crumpled papers and morphine?"

"Fuck."

Harry Kay's old stopwatch was in box 627. As I stumbled outdoors, mist poured over Blue Mountain's crater summit like a roaring waterfall. On the backside of Harry Kay's letter was a map of the Tunnels.

The cop said, "Use your brain this time."

I nodded. After memorizing the map, I dropped the paper on the muddy street in a crackling flame.

THIRTY-TWO
First Win

"Last chance to tie your shoelaces, boys."

Loitering in the muddy streets of Lake of the Woods, I played our secret game from Organ Pipe, using myself as bait. Soon my crisscrossed tracks gained another set of prints. Mr. Cuddy was in hot pursuit.

I said, "Into the web, Old Paint."

Slipping into the timber, I hiked along the edge of Iris Ridge and then knifed between the 27 giant Jeffreys. At the center of the burnt-out area was the lone Jeffrey pine. During my performance, I stole glances under my arm but could never spot him. He was too clever to allow me to see his position. Didn't matter, though, I sensed his presence.

Anticipating Mr. Cuddy's approach, I squirmed under the dirt and pulled out Harry Kay's stopwatch. No fuck-ups. The brush above my head crackled with his preternatural radar.

"You ought to be ashamed," the cop who shot himself scolded.

"What for?"

"Toying with an old man."

"Mr. Cuddy is no ordinary old man."

"Last chance to tie your shoelaces, boys," the L.A. city official bellowed over his bullhorn.

Dunham said, "I loathe that man."

"Hey, Kay," J. said. "Help me eyeball Taft."

Larson said, "No different than running laps around the coffee table."

The official starter raised a vintage double-barreled shotgun. I said, "Good Lord, nice piece."

KABLAM. Bolting from my hospital bed, which Julie Christie had equipped with a starting block, I galloped across the burnt-out area with a huge head start. Mr. Cuddy slipped out his own shotgun and blasted two rounds.

"False start, boys," he said over the bullhorn. "False start."

I hollered over my shoulder, "Nice try, Mr. Cuddy." In the game everything was a trick.

Approaching the entrance to Tunnels, I skidded to a halt and scanned the perimeter. Not a single spook or enemy runner from Taft in sight.

"Concentrate on style."

"Set the course on fire, Kay," Coach Godfrey roared from the sidelines.

I swooped into Harry Kay's Tunnels. The walls and ceiling of branches revolved with such velocity my vision blurred with the colors of Hughes Supermarket on Balboa and Devonshire. The jarring in my knees and hip faded. My feet no longer tapped the ground.

Arching my back, I banked off Butterscotch Creek like a surfer dropping into a twelve-foot Rincon peak. Its momentum spit me across Iris Ridge to Maray Point. Slapping the great southern oak, I hurtled off the edge and landed aboard my Schwinn ten-speed from Woodly Hill. My thumb punched Harry Kay's stopwatch.

Mr. Cuddy staggered from the woods with his back to the road. He was breathless and searching

Iris Ridge with binoculars. This was a delicious moment. Raising my pocket camera, I took careful aim and snapped his picture.

He sighed and, without turning around, said, "Hello, Garrett."

"Hey, Mr. Cuddy. Quite a day."

"A bit too warm." It was still forty-seven degrees on the porch post.

"Could get warmer."

"No, cold front is coming." But he bowed slightly as if to acknowledge my victory.

"Cold fronts no longer intimidate me," I said through clenched teeth.

"Perhaps." He nodded with genuine respect. "Would you still like to hike with me on Blue Mountain? North slope is my territory. Maybe I can show you something new."

"It would be an honor," I said, without paying much attention. Too busy relishing my first win.

"Tomorrow morning?"

"Fine."

It may have been sly to develop my film, but I had a comic notion, dwelling upon mirrors and Christopher Lee, that no image would appear in the photo.

THIRTY-THREE
The Grassy Circle

Mr. Cuddy uses a pogo stick.

The profile of Mr. Cuddy appeared in the window, ringed by the orange porch light. He rapped lightly on the kitchen door.

"It's never locked."

Toting the vintage shotgun under his long gray overcoat, he stomped on the wooden porch and tossed my key back on the roof.

"Morning."

I said, "Take off your bandit coat and sit by the fire. It's putting out some good heat."

"Thanks, but I prefer the cold."

"Coffee?"

"If it's lukewarm."

"I'll add an ice cube. Honey?"

"Okay."

"Muffins?"

"No, thank you." His voice had the malicious drawl of Jack Palance. "I never eat before hiking Blue Mountain." He slumped into a chair at the kitchen table and sipped his coffee. "What was that little joke you made up in Valley Hospital?"

"Can't piss. There must be a chili bean stuck up my dick."

"No, the other one."

"Am I high or is this how it feels to die?"

Mr. Cuddy looked me over. "Blue Mountain can be quite unnerving."

I said, "No, she's exquisite."

"You relish surprises."

"I'm a Christopher Lee fan."

"I read Harry Kay's letter."

"Letter?"

"C'mon, Garrett. I'm postmaster in Lake of the Woods."

"He said to forget about him."

"Harry Kay doesn't want you distracted." Mr. Cuddy put down his cup and strolled to the door. Slitting the curtains with a long finger, he peered out the window. It was nine degrees on the porch post. "Told you it was a cold front."

I nodded. "You promised to show me something new on the north slope."

He glanced at the orange porch light above the kitchen door. "Don't you want to turn off your light?"

"I like it to burn in case I'm in the woods after dark."

"Won't last long."

"Hasn't flickered yet."

At the end of the paved road, Mr. Cuddy led me to a remote arm of Iris Ridge and attacked a difficult slope on his hands and knees. At his age, I never expected him to attempt this section of Blue Mountain. Although sweating profusely, I experienced trouble with the cold. It seemed to freeze my joints. My cowardly brooding returned with a vengeance. It was beyond dreadful. I desperately needed my shot of morphine. I wished I hadn't tagged along with Mr. Cuddy. Considering the intensity of my recent training, my legs appeared woefully out of shape.

While Mr. Cuddy labored effortlessly, I glared at the back of his head and cursed his vigor. Not once did he look back to witness my obvious struggling. Bastard wasn't human. Without warning he slammed on the brakes and caught me by surprise. I stumbled into his ribs.

"Oof," he said.

"Sorry."

"You're not paying attention. Thought you were a patrol leader."

"Paying attention has never been a strong point. My mind wanders. You brought me up here to show me something. Okay, show me."

Mr. Cuddy grinned. "Sense of humor is your best weapon."

"You're trying to confuse me."

"Don't you recognize this grassy circle?"

"Yeah, so?"

He pointed to a clump of bushes. Initially, I didn't comprehend. Then I became nauseous. He was pointing to the bottom entrance of the Tunnels. After fifty years, Mr. Cuddy had finally discovered Harry Kay's secret passage and I was entirely to blame. My shoulders drooped visibly. His new grin was malicious and terrifying.

"Harry Kay was fast. He had speed and natural grace. At the age of twenty-seven, after a steam shovel had crushed his chest, Harry Kay used this tunnel to whip me down Blue Mountain. At seventy-seven, he politely declined a rematch. Then his grandson appears on Blue Mountain preparing for war."

"Stop it, Mr. Cuddy."

"Only the Tunnels is not your way, it was Harry Kay's. You must race down Blue Mountain using your own path. You have speed and natural grace. But you're violent and unpredictable, much more formidable than Harry Kay. I admit you frighten me."

"Yeah, right."

"Although you may not realize it, I'm certain you have designed your own course."

"No, I haven't."

"What are you doing in Lake of the Woods?"

"It's my home."

"You live at the San Franciscan apartments in Sepulveda."

"Not any longer, Mr. Cuddy. I moved. Besides, my friends have visited me here."

"Only friends from the accident."

"You're not from the accident."

"I am the accident."

"No."

Mr. Cuddy rested his hand on my shoulder. "Garrett, when did Harry Kay die? Before or after the trip to Organ Pipe?"

"Before," I said, firmly. "Dunham and I spoke of Harry Kay the night before Organ Pipe."

"Dunham and you spoke of Harry Kay in Lake of the Woods."

"Yes, that's true."

"Why didn't you go to Harry Kay's funeral?"

"Because…" I experienced mental anguish. I became incoherent. "I--I'm too selfish. I wanted to go, but didn't want to spend the time or money."

Mr. Cuddy said, "Stop trying to feel guilty. Harry Kay died on the day of your accident at Hughes Supermarket, November 8, 1974. He was broken by his grief."

"What grief?"

"He was informed of your ridiculous accident."

"Why would Harry Kay suffer from grief? I'm alive."

"You're in combat, and Dr. Kildare advised him you were losing badly."

I said, "Wrong again. What's so terrible about my accident? I'm okay now. Recovered, said the nasty cashier."

"What is this place called Blue Mountain?"

"I'll know when she tells me."

"Kay…"

"No more, Mr. Cuddy. Leave me alone. You're just a spook from Elvira's Fright Night."

Charging down the most vertical slope on Iris Ridge, I was numb and wobbly. My roller coasters were sloppy. In the corner of my eye, I noticed Mr. Cuddy loping alongside mimicking my strides. He surged around a manzanita and managed to cut underneath and avert my concentration. I struck the ground in an awkward position and slid on my chest, colliding with a Jeffrey pine.

Squinting into the dust, I watched Mr. Cuddy bounce away on what appeared to
be a pogo stick.

"Good Lord," I said. "Impressive."

THIRTY-FOUR
No More Beliefs Forever

*If in need of a good cry,
look up Chief Joseph of the Nez Perce.*

My left calf had a bloody bone bruise with the imprint of Mr. Cuddy's pogo stick. Dr. Kildare owed me another Purple Heart. Swatting dust and pine bark off my Pendleton, I searched the banks of Butterscotch Creek for Hughes Supermarket. No one had swept up the pile of broken glass from the freezer door. In the refrigerated air, the aroma of ripe and defrosting food was suffocating.

Once again, my perception was suspect. Morphine was playing tricks. Underneath my silver bracelet, the morning's fresh needle mark was pink and sore. All the explanations and beliefs I had invented to retain my image of the world had been plundered. Blue Mountain had snipped my anchor.

"Wha-aaat?" snapped the nurse over the intercom.

I said, "Do me a favor. I want you to thank the cop who shot himself."

"Thank him for what?"

"Thank him for reminding me of Chief Joseph."

"Chief who?"

"Chief Joseph was a Nez Perce who fled to Canada, but was captured by the Seventh Cavalry near the border."

"Hmm...that clears it up."

"From where the sun now stands, I will have no more beliefs forever."

THIRTY-FIVE
That Evening

Kay decides to play the game with Cary Grant.

That evening my rustic cabin acquired personality; it was warm and cheery with a foolish grin. In the potbelly stove a stack of piñón logs crackled and spit. Using a chilled glass of chardonnay, I dabbed the newest needle mark under my silver bracelet while savoring the buzz in my testicles.

The CBS Late Show was about to get under way. On the sunny Riviera, Cary Grant and a Pink Panther were about to burglarize a sleek mansion.

It was time to swing into action. Following a strict "lights out" policy, with the hope that Mr. Cuddy would be dozing at his listening post, I put on my L.L. Bean hiking boots and smeared my face with Carolina ash. Cary Grant added the finishing touches.

"We could be brothers," he said in a delightful voice.

"It takes a thief, Mr. Grant."

Creeping into town on my belly, I used the lights from Hampton's Village Market as my source of reference. Hampton's was still open for business, minus Mrs. Hampton and her Buffalo beer. Darting across Frazier Mountain Highway, I slipped between the post office and May West Realty. I crouched in the alley and checked the orange night clock while maintaining intercom silence. Mission on schedule.

No Mr. Cuddy on my trail tonight. Feeling my way along the back of May West, I slowly approached the Cuddy Ski and Toboggan Rental Shop. A sturdy chain-link fence fortressed the grounds. Without causing a major ruckus, I wedged my big toe into a square and scaled the fence to its razor crown. Nasty barbs were pronged and rusty. Stretching the top wire with my left hand, I managed to grip an edge of the roof and sling myself into the compound

"Fuck me," I cried.

Lighting a match, I discovered two deep punctures in perfect formation with my other needle marks. A thin line of blood streamed from both wounds.

Inside the shop I fondled the goods, but they were either too long or clumsy. On the last shelf was the object of my desire. Though built for two, it was ideal for the job. Snatching it from the rack, I crept to the back door and entered the alley. Before leaving, I checked the door to make certain it was locked from the inside. No fuck-ups.

Crawling home on my belly, I dragged the toboggan by its nose. A black Labrador trotted across Frazier Mountain Highway and hopped over the concrete marker.

I lifted my head. "Woody!"

My orange porch light was still shining. Cabin's personality remained warm and cheery. There was the attractive option of settling into my rocker with another glass of chardonnay, or planting my new toboggan on Blue Mountain.

Wondered if Woody would enjoy a trip to Butterscotch Creek.

THIRTY-SIX
Decoy

*Granada Hills coach Giles Godfrey
was a fiend for time trials.*

Mr. Cuddy had been twice correct. On my porch post the temperature had remained fixed at nine degrees. More significantly, I had indeed designed my own course down Blue Mountain.

It had finally registered. Standing on the Lab's concrete marker for the last time, I recalled studying the maze of trails from the edge of Mt. Pinos. At that moment a trail with huge testicles had boldly revealed itself.

Armed with Harry Kay's stopwatch, I ascended Blue Mountain in Tunnels in order to rid myself of Mr. Cuddy. It hadn't taken me long to realize Tunnels was still taboo to him.

No map this time.

Dividing the course into seven fragments, I stuffed them into a special drawer. Mr. Cuddy had power, but he couldn't pry into my brain.

During seven dusty time trials to the paved road, I randomly created a route, with the exception of one fragment of my secret course. Harry Kay's stopwatch was punched at that precise moment. The remaining interval of my run was used as a decoy. Although I never saw him, Mr. Cuddy's presence in the Tehachapi's was quite obvious. Perhaps he was armed with his video camera and preparing another contribution to *Mutual of Omaha's Wild Kingdom*.

During my seven practice runs I scouted the mountain for possible escape routes. I also wondered if Mr. Cuddy had been friends with Marlin Perkins.

Amid the Jeffrey pines at the center of Blue Mountain's crater summit sat two freshly piled sand mounds. Flapping in the breeze was a banner that read START in big blue letters. It was a sure bet that a finish chute sat on the paved road. My initial step in the game was crucial. No margin for hesitation or weakness, because it would set the mood for the entire performance.

Damn shoelaces must be tied.

First section—Blue Mountain's crater summit. From my own sand mound a faint path led to the four-foot rim encircling the summit in direct line with Mt. Pinos and Lake Buena Vista. These were the lost mine coordinates. With proper timing, a fortunate leap off the rim would pitch me on top of my hidden toboggan.

Second section—burnt-out area. It was in the burnt-out area where I intended to fool Mr. Cuddy and take command. Since his strategy depended on contact, he would be waiting in the manzanita for my next move. Using the slick ice and mud, I could skid under Mr. Cuddy's radar and reach the timber long before he realized he had been duped.

He'd probably counter with his pogo stick.

Third section—Tunnels. Feigning toward the upper entrance, I counted on Mr. Cuddy's defensive play pending my use of Harry Kay's Tunnels. If Mr. Cuddy fell for my ruse and took his own shortcut, he'd be at the wrong place when I emerged from the flats.

Fourth section—legendary 27 giant Jeffreys and Butterscotch Creek. It was a macabre and intense setting that seemed destined to be a turning point. I remembered my stored mental notes. Sometimes Butterscotch Creek had water and other times it was dry. Also, Butterscotch Creek could outrun me.

Fifth section—hills. A series of sharp hills led to Iris Ridge. If Mr. Cuddy managed a lead by this point, I planned to destroy him on the hills. Hill running was my specialty during the '64 cross-country campaign.

Sixth section—Iris Ridge. Whacking the great southern oak on Maray Point, its trunk tattooed with a disturbing likeness of Mr. Cuddy or Jack Palance, had the potential of being the highlight of my race.

Seventh section—paved road. If I had the slightest lead, no mule deer or 77-year-old Los Padres ranger could whip me down the final thousand feet to the paved road.

With Harry Kay's stopwatch I had timed my reckless victory using Tunnels. After my week of training, I added the individual times of the seven fragments of the new course. My way was a clean 27 seconds faster.

THIRTY-SEVEN
The Orange Porch Light
(Is On)

Larson's secret strategy comes to the rescue.

In celebration of my seventh and final time trial, following an elegant supper from Hampton's Village Market (and soothing bath with no cloudy urine or hiking boots, thank you), I lounged in the rocker with a glass of chardonnay. I couldn't stop thinking about Mr. Cuddy.

Without warning my lousy, despicable fear crept into room 9 and sneered.

Dr. Kildare said, "Set up your ambush, Kay."

"Yes, sir."

"Do it now."

Larson's best cure for Sierra del Ajo was summoned. He would rarely resort to laps around a dopey coffee table.

November's chill turned warm and breezy, resembling a summer eve in the San Fernando Valley. Inspired by the promise of a teenage rendezvous, I roared into a Granada Hills haze, deploying my favorite shortcut across the Hughes Supermarket parking lot with its scattered shopping carts and broken glass. In Northridge, near Lassen and Encino, I cruised by Julie Christie's house. Her orange porch light blinked twice.

Obeying strict field instructions, my battered 340 Duster chugged around a corner and parked in the back alley. Muscling over her brick wall, I smelled sea and butterscotch blowing in from the Ventura coast. Sliding screen door was unlocked.

Julie Christie was waiting and prepared in her parents' master bedroom. An owl-shade lamp sat on a night table. In its soft glow, I spied her blue panties and small upturned breasts.

I said, "This is better than I imagined."

She giggled. "You don't know yet."

"Sure looks better."

"Then don't turn off the light."

Outside the bedroom, a tray of blood samples jingled. Strolling down the hall with a faint smile on her lips, the *real* Julie Christie snapped the plastic off a hypodermic syringe. When her nurse's uniform sank to the carpet, lush red Olympia neon hair melted underneath my chest. Nice trick! Instead of my first Julie Christie, I was having sex with nurse Julie Christie.

Moments later there was a stiff sensation in my left hip. When I attempted to look under the sheet, Julie Christie pressed her warm mouth over mine and injected morphine. Her moist fingers combed the left side of my hair.

It was November in the Tehachapi's and both Julie Christies had long absconded. But not my erection. Clenching my fist, I said, "Yeah, Larson."

There was a startling thud on my wooden porch. Without hesitation I flew to the TV and hid behind the rabbit ears. Charlton Heston had just bopped an unfortunate cowboy on the head with a frying pan.

My orange porch light had been extinguished. From the TV, I glimpsed myself in the rocker with a deflated but blazing penis. Racing into the kitchen, I yanked open the door and discovered my bulb had been deliberately unscrewed. On the wooden porch was a leather bag and double-barreled shotgun in mint condition. Leather bag contained 27 magnum shells and a queen of hearts.

I twisted back the bulb. "Not very subtle, Mr. Cuddy."

THIRTY-EIGHT
Organ Pipe

*Larson was correct about
Organ Pipe National Monument.*

After sprucing up Mr. Cuddy's antique shotgun, I treated myself to another soak in the tub with a tall glass of chardonnay. My fresh needle mark was pink and sore.

"You fought bravely, Kay," Dr. Kildare said over the intercom.

"Friendly casualties?"

"None."

"Will that trend continue?"

"Not indefinitely."

"Why?"

He walked into the room. "Don't concern yourself with losses. It's a major distraction.

"I don't understand."

Dr. Kildare lowered my chart. "Listen, you've been a fine patient. That's the best you can be under the circumstances."

"I know I've been a coward."

"Not true. You've taken some genuine shit. With the exception of that little squabble in the emergency room, you've been one helluva wiseass."

"You've been a fine medic."

"I know I've caused you distress."

I said, "Not true. You care about your people. The cop who shot himself and I agree that when Dr. Kildare walks into room nine the world is in its proper place."

"Don't back down from that old bastard, Kay."

"Mr. Cuddy?"

"Mr. Whoever."

In a surge of hot morphine, I located Organ Pipe National Monument. Behind the ranger station was an arroyo that wound for miles to the lifeless butte of Sierra del Ajo. Barbed cholla and an army of organ pipe peppered the rolling hills.

I said, "Bleak panorama."

"We don't see the complete picture," Larson said.

J. tossed my leather coat with no buttons into the backseat of the 340 Duster. "Bullshit." He glanced towards Sierra del Ajo. "I see the complete picture."

Larson said, "No, you don't."

"Yeah, I do."

"What's around the bend in that arroyo?"

"Same as this shit."

"Not likely, J."

"It's all the same, Larson."

"Nothing is the same." Larson looked at me. "Prove it, Kay. Check out the arroyo."

"Larson, please. We've got an emergency. You're hurt bad. I'm serious. It's a two-hour drive to Gila Bend."

"Humor me, Garrett."

Around the bend in the arroyo, glistening with the prongs of cholla and organ pipe, was an achingly beautiful desolation. "Same shit," I said, "only different." I scanned the perimeter for Edward Abbey.

"What are you doing, Loco Loco?" the cop who shot himself said. "I see you behind the TV."

"When did they bring you back to room nine?"

"I'm not in room nine. This is the recovery room."

"Are you recovered?"

He shrugged. "Doctors are still mum."

"Maybe I can read your chart."

"No, please don't. I don't want to know until they tell me."

"What are you staring at?"

"You. You're hopping on the TV like Ricochet Rabbit."

Perhaps I had finally acquired Mr. Cuddy's pogo trick. I hopped across the Sonora in search of jellies and hot mud. In time, I lost track of the places I had visited or what occurred. Only the hopping mattered.

Larson said, "What'd you find, Kay?"

"Same shit, right?" said J.

I said, "It appears to me Sierra del Ajo is Blue Mountain with a mustache."

THIRTY-NINE
The Orange Porch Light
(Is Off)

The sky continues to be moist and sticky.

With respect for Tehachapi tradition, I timed my departure from Lake of the Woods to coincide with the sun settling on the head of Mt. Pinos. At that precise moment, J. and I were known to challenge the fates.

In a quickie tour, I reviewed all my possessions in the cabin. Solid wood rocker and owl-shade lamp sat next to a comfy sofa. Potbelly stove. Rabbit-eared TV and Navajo rug. In the bathroom was the claw-foot tub with a fresh urine bottle. In the frigid writing room was an oak secretary with my crumpled papers and morphine. For luck, I stuffed the petrified rock from Organ Pipe National Monument into my pocket.

My favorite place was the wooden porch with its temperature post and orange porch light. The 340 Duster sat under the carport.

With the exception of a flask of chardonnay—"to kill the chill"—all sedations were stashed in a desk drawer. In response to Mr. Cuddy's prediction, the temperature in Lake of the Woods hadn't budged from nine degrees. In Harry Kay's Tunnels, those wintry moans from the Pacific would be merciless.

Weighted down with Mr. Cuddy's shotgun and leather bag of shells, I meticulously assaulted the western edge of Iris Ridge, and then relaxed under the great southern oak at Maray Point. My fingers caressed her rigid bark.

Riding a blast of wind, several pine cones sailed into a sky that was moist and sticky, resembling the blue honey at Balboa and Devonshire.

Every hair on my body stiffened. Wrestling with my dismal inclination to brood, I refused to become unnerved. Somewhere in the bush, Mr. Cuddy was watching me as I leaned against the great southern oak.

Where was he hiding?

As chardonnay spilled over my chin, I was astonished to discover that Blue Mountain had developed an alluring and seductive beauty.

I grinned. "We've had a few dates." The imperfection of its burnt scar gave Blue Mountain a female quality that intensified her charm and sexiness.

At the entrance to Harry Kay's Tunnels, taboo for Mr. Cuddy, I looked down Iris Ridge and noticed a few lights flickering in the misty town of Lake of the Woods. I couldn't find my little cabin. Though its location was most familiar, I couldn't spot my orange porch light.

Holy shit! The bulb must have finally expired.

FORTY
Harry Kay

*"Quien es?" Billy the Kid said at Fort Sumner.
It was Pat Garrett.*

I brushed aside the branches to Harry Kay's Tunnels and an icy breath from the Pacific moaned in my ear. It was a cruel and sobering whisper.

I said, "Minne-fucking-sota weather."

Flipping my collar, I shook out my hair and took another deep draw of chardonnay. After three or four gulps, wine poured out the corners of my mouth and streamed down my chin.

"Hey, Dun."

"Wha-aat?" He was still irritated with me because Half Dome resembled the Empire State Building.

"Might help if you don't look down."

"Listen to Sir Edmund Hillary. Hey, you're splashing water in my face."

I laughed. "Nope, it's chardonnay."

Rather than scrambling up Tunnels in my usual fashion, I focused on style, as if each gesture might be my final one. For an encore, I swallowed a few more mouthfuls of chardonnay and chased it with water. Despite the horrendous cold, the alcohol began to work its magic.

"Mr. Cuddy will use your friends to distract you," Tunnels said in a familiar voice.

"*Quien es?*" I said. "Who is that?"

My grandfather, Harry Kay, leaned on a piñón pine. "Took you long enough to get here, kid. I'm freezing."

"Jesus Christ."

Harry Kay glanced behind the piñón just to make certain. "No, it's only Grandpa."

"Wish I had another flask of chardonnay."

"I've something with a little more authority."

"Mr. Cuddy predicted you would come to Blue Mountain."

"Think of me as another bandit on the rim."

I said, "Harry, sorry I revealed Tunnels to Mr. Cuddy."

"It was my mistake," he said, pouring our whisky. "Should have known you'd discover a quicker way."

I nodded.

"Listen to me, Garrett. Counter Mr. Cuddy's distractions with your own tricks."

"What tricks?"

"Jokes, for instance. Am I high or this how it feels to die?"

"What are my other tricks?"

"Your friends, Dunham and J."

"Is Dunham here?"

"He's under the chili beans."

I looked down aisle 9. "I remember now."

"Dunham accepts what happens and moves on."

I said, "Harry, I've planted a toboggan."

"Mr. Cuddy will be very cautious. He won't gamble because he's scared of you and J."

"Why?"

"J. personifies controlled violence."

167

"Where is J.?"

"He's sitting by the *TV Guide* and gum rack."

"Harry," I stammered. A wave of nausea washed over me. "I must confess I'm petrified."

"Without fear you wouldn't be worth shit."

"How do I deal with Mr. Cuddy?"

"Remember, no hesitations."

"Gone with the gun."

"No regrets."

"None with much bite."

"Good boy," he said, loading up his pack. "It's time for me to return to Lake Vermillion."

"Wait, Gramps. Stay."

"It's my home, son. Your home is Lake of the Woods."

"Please," I begged, "don't go."

"I'll come back after you whip Mr. Cuddy."

"Hey, Harry. With any luck, someone is going to receive a swift kick to the gonads."

"All mangled up and he's still a wiseass."

With minimal effort, shades of Crazy Legs Hirsh, I quickened my pace while crisscrossing Harry Kay's Tunnels. Striding across the burnt-out area, head bobbing above the brush, I noticed the sun hadn't sunk behind the western Tehachapi's. At the edge of Blue Mountain's crater summit, the sun's lip still peeked over somber Mt. Pinos.

Blindly, I had won. Instead of groping wildly, I had whipped the sunset by upping my panache.

FORTY-ONE
Mr. Cuddy

*Just because you're dead,
it doesn't mean you don't exist.*

Mr. Cuddy's Start banner rippled in a sudden gust of Pacific spray. Stepping up to the sand mound, I shut my eyes and remembered the hoopla of L.A.'s 1964 Cross Country City Championship.

My teammates were the key, I decided. At the starting line, surrounded by the colors and snarls of 160 enemy troops, it was difficult to keep the vomit from leaping up my throat.

"Not today, you Granada fucks," they hissed.

"Go home, girls."

As officials blabbed ad nauseam over loudspeakers, a mob of unruly spectators took up positions on the Pierce College course in anticipation of the varsity finals.

I said, "Every team has a hatchet man assigned to Granada Hills."

"Let me elbow our way through the pack," J. volunteered. J. was controlled violence.

"I can't handle losing to Taft or Lincoln. I'm so scared of losing."

"Most of them believe we're going to win, Kay," Dunham said. "But win or lose, we still surf Rincon in the morning." Dunham had already accepted victory— or possible defeat—and made plans to move on.

"I'm too nervous."

"They all wipe their butts the same way," Larson growled. Larson had such bravado as a teenager.

So what was my role? We had fire, acceptance, and intrepidness. What could I possibly contribute to a marked varsity team burdened all season with the curse of "defending champion"?

With somber theatrics, in full view of the entire field, I motioned for a Granada huddle. In the next moment, the pre-race gibberish was muffled. Enemy runners stared quietly, almost respectfully.

"LAST CHANCE TO TIE YOUR SHOELACES, ASSHOLES," I bellowed in a flawless impersonation of the scruffy old starter.

"Garrett."

Whirling to my left, fists in the air, I found him squatting on the other sand mound. "Hello, Mr. Cuddy."

"Brought my pogo stick," he said.

I smiled. "Can't frighten me today."

"I don't presume."

"Nor I."

Mr. Cuddy said, "What do you want to know about Blue Mountain?"

"I don't understand."

"Ask me a question."

"Okay…WHO ARE YOU?" I shouted.

"You know who I am."

"No, I don't," I insisted. "Well, maybe." The accident and the game. Harry Kay.

Blue Mountain began to smell like Hughes Supermarket.

"What do you think is happening?"

"Mr. Cuddy, I…I believe I'm dying."

"No, you're not," Mr. Cuddy said. "You're fighting. And you're such a fine warrior, you've challenged and even spooked your own death."

"What are you talking about?"

"Blue Mountain, me, all this." He waved his hand through the blue honey.

I lay on the cold tile floor of Hughes Supermarket with broken glass on my chest. Vampires from the *TV Guide* and gum rack hovered in the aisle. Julie Christie and Henry the dog vet peered over Larson's shoulder.

I said to Larson, "Mr. Cuddy just paid me a compliment. I'm spooking Sierra del Ajo." A grin larger than the Cheshire Cat's appeared on Larson's face.

"Whip the bastard down Blue Mountain," he said.

"What about this relic?" I asked, gripping the double-barreled shotgun. "Do I need it?"

Mr. Cuddy said, "You're in combat. It's the L.A. City Finals on Blue Mountain. There may be a gunfight. Anything is possible on Blue Mountain."

"Victory?"

"If you win, you live for another day or seventy years. If you lose, you move on. In Lake of the Woods, there is no difference."

"What's the purpose?"

"Don't be too concerned with purpose, Garrett. Life and death are equal."

I nodded.

Mr. Cuddy pulled out his movie camera. In his eye was the twinkle of Jack Palance. "It's all being recorded on the cosmic film."

"You're not a bad old dude," I said.

"Runners—take your mark," the old starter commanded.

Mr. Cuddy said, "I must warn you. I've planted some tricks on Blue Mountain."

"You'll notice my counterpunches."

"Violence and acceptance, I suppose."

"Maybe some jokes."

"Of course, you're a wiseass."

"Just out of curiosity, do you ever run into Duster on Blue Mountain?"

He tilted his head. "You've seen Woody, haven't you?"

I sucked in my breath. "When did the 28th giant Jeffrey fall?"

"June 21, 1947."

"Why must people die?"

"To make life precious, if anyone bothers to notice."

"What will happen if I die?"

"Just because you're dead, it doesn't mean you don't exist."

"Runners—set."

"By the way," he said. "The cop who shot himself has recovered. In a few months he'll be running and jumping over fences for the Van Nuys police department."

Now it was my turn to gloat. Mr. Cuddy should have never admitted that to me. When I attempted to speak, he held up his hand, but I asked anyway, "Are you a Los Padres ranger?"

His eyes slid into their right corners and squinted. "Remember the wolf?"

"Sure."

"Anything is possible on Blue Mountain," he repeated.

FORTY-TWO
Queen of Hearts

Only the performance mattered.

Slipping Mr. Cuddy's antique shotgun from its leather holster, I closed my eyes and squeezed both triggers. KABLAM KABLAM. As magnum pellets scattered into a red sky, the gun kicked out of my hand.

Standing under our START banner was the tyrannical yet jovial Giles Godfrey, coach of the Granada Hills champion cross-country teams.

I said, "Hey, Coach."

"Hey, Number One."

"What are you doing on the rim?"

"Seems like a good place to spot bandits."

"I'm glad you're here, Coach."

"Listen to me, Kay," he said, fiercely. Then his tone became paternal. "I want you to really uncork one."

My hospital phone buzzed. "Hello?"

A woman whispered, "Is this Garret Kay?"

"I'm kind of in the middle of something."

"This is Ms. D."

"Pardon?"

"Ms. D.," she repeated. "I drove the black Seville."

"Where are you calling from?"

"Hughes Supermarket. The crabby cashier brought me her work phone."

"Probably still bitching about my New and Improved Tums."

Ms. D. said, "It's true. You are a wiseass."

I said, "I'm glad we can talk. Larson didn't mean to be so rough."

"I want you to accept my apology."

"No apology necessary."

"Perhaps if I explained."

"The cop who shot himself told me the whole story."

She said, "I still feel guilty."

"Apology accepted, then. I'm sorry too."

"What for?"

"For haranguing you at the freezer door."

"I would have said worse."

"I also feel real bad about…"

"About?"

"Woody."

With an incredible surge, Mr. Cuddy crossed the crater summit to its four-foot rim. In my head was a dazzling image of Joaquin Murrieta campground on Mt. Pinos with the queen of hearts stuck in a fire grill.

Garrett Kay, June 21, 1947—November 8, 1974 was written on the card. Didn't say much, but I was satisfied.

Winning or losing had no meaning. Only the performance mattered.

FORTY-THREE
Blue Mountain

Kay looks into the eyes of the Seville.

Lingering on Blue Mountain's crater summit, last bandit on the rim, I waited for a recall blast or whistle, but it had been a fair start. The silver bracelet from Mission de San Fernando clung desperately to my wrist.

"*Pequeña belleza,*" I said tenderly. "You can go home again."

It sparkled thrice when it was frisbeed over the crater.

With his head popping above the chaparral, Mr. Cuddy bounced into the burnt-out area using his pogo stick. With each hop he glanced over his shoulder to check on my progress. I was busy playing a craftier version of our hide and go seek nonsense.

Trailing from a safe distance, I slipped into the burnt-out area and located my plot of fresh dirt. In seconds the toboggan shifted into high gear. The slope was in mint icy condition. Gripping the reins, I pushed onto a deer trail and skidded out of control. Unintentionally, the toboggan's upturned nose plowed into Mr. Cuddy's pogo stick.

I said, "*Adios,* Hopalong."

But this toboggan was born and bred at Cuddy Ski and Toboggan Rentals, and was no Benedict

Arnold. When Mr. Cuddy issued a sharp whistle, I was promptly bucked into the mud and manzanita.

"Lucky I enjoy a lead," I said to the toboggan, "or you would be introduced to Mr. Potbelly Stove."

Veering toward Harry Kay's Tunnels, it was time to play my first decoy. In the shadows I heard the sound of clicking spikes. Someone was in hot pursuit.

"Mr. Cuddy recovered quickly," I said, astonished. Ducking behind a Jeffrey, I prepared to trip him with the butt of his own shotgun. But no one appeared.

I peeked around the trunk and saw J. at the top of the slope poised with his Colt's. At Organ Pipe, J. had been the first to return to the giant saguaro.

"Hey, Kay."

I said, "I remember now. You and I were standing together at the *TV Guide* and gum rack."

"We could be twins."

I smiled. "Blue Mountain brothers."

"Hauled Larson's ass off Sierra del Ajo."

"Whipped the traffic on Woodly Hill."

"Serenaded by a wolf." J. was shifting me into a dangerous mood.

"Survived a gunfight at Sespe Creek."

"What?"

"Drank some fine chardonnay."

"Damn cheap chardonnay."

I said, "J., it was broken glass from Hughes Supermarket that nicked your throat."

"Sorry about your leather coat," he said, tossing me the buttons.

"You're hurt bad," I said. "Why don't you come to Valley Hospital?"

He shrugged. "Too busy playing the game. I think you grabbed the lead with that toboggan."

"With any luck, Mr. Cuddy fell for my decoy and is guarding the entrance to Harry Kay's Tunnels."

"Why are you hiding behind the tree, Kay?"

"No reason."

"Let me see you."

"Okay." I stepped out from behind the Jeffrey.

He said, "Doesn't matter who goes on from here."

"What do you mean?"

"For one of us the game is over."

As he raised his Colt's, I licked a drop of blood from my nose. The instant he fired, a shopping cart from Hughes Supermarket slammed into my hip and saved my life. The bullet sloshed sloppily through my right shoulder, kicking me into the air. Mr. Cuddy's shotgun flew from its holster and clattered down the rocks, but I managed to hang onto the leather bag and scramble behind another tree.

In place of the shopping cart was a lean Chicano with bullet belt and sombrero.

I said, "Who are you?"

"Murrieta, *amigo*. Joaquin Murrieta."

"*El Bandido?*"

"At your service."

"Why did you help me?"

"You have made a deep impression," he said.

I tilted my head. "How could I possibly impress the most famous bandit in California history?"

He said, "During your stay with us, you have shown the Tehachapi's much respect. Little red-haired *muchacha es muy simpatica tambien*."

"I'm honored. Joaquin Murrieta is my favorite Tehachapi legend."

"*Gracias, Senor* Kay."

Blood oozed from a bullet hole thicker than my thumb. "This is incorrect," I said. "My shoulder wasn't injured at Hughes Supermarket."

Larson said, "You're wrong." His hands were drenched with my blood. "You demolished a steak knife display in aisle nine."

"Of course, our killing knives."

In the dirt, Mr. Cuddy's shotgun was cracked open and ready to load. Carefully I reached into the leather bag and selected two shells.

J. said, "Come out, Garrett. It's your turn. Nick me on the throat."

"No way, J."

"Don't waste precious time."

"No," I said.

Poking my petrified rock from Organ Pipe National Monument around the Jeffrey, I spotted J., still in a shooter's crouch with his Colt's raised. KAPOW. Petrified rock disintegrated in my hand. "Damn, J., you killed my rock." Snatching the shotgun, I popped in both shells.

He said, "You gotta fight, Garrett."

"Why?"

"It's your nature."

"But you're the tough guy."

"You're tough too. You're also unpredictable."

Resting a hand on the tree, I steadied my vertigo and focused. In the game everything was a trick. As a counterpunch, I emerged from the left side.

"Try again," J. said, his eyes fixed to the right. "Shoot the damn gun."

I hesitated.

"Do it," he insisted.

KABLAM. The butt rammed against my wounded shoulder. "Christ," I said. J. was blown into cash register nine, ripping the buttons off my leather coat. It was fortunate that the crabby cashier had departed. This Seville was taking no prisoners. His body crumpled to the tile floor, peppered with bloodied pieces of glass. Didn't faze J. With a sly grin, he brushed himself off.

He said, "When the medics arrive, don't let them forget me. I'm going to need a load of stitches."

"See you in the ambulance."

"Set the course on fire, Kay."

Near the entrance to Tunnels, the 27 giant Jeffreys towered four times higher than any other tree in the Los Padres National Forest. They could be seen clearly from Frazier Mountain Highway. In a careless moment, admiring the tall branches, I stumbled and punched my nose into the icy snow. More blood flowed. The blow helped me recall my stored mental notes about Butterscotch Creek. Then I discovered what had grabbed my foot. Jutting from the ground was the corner to a thick iron door. "Monks'," I said. It was the entrance to the fabled Mission de San Fernando mine.

Mr. Cuddy's secret spot was marked by the 27 giant Jeffries. Picture was clear now. On June 21, 1947, the 28th giant Jeffrey splintered over

Butterscotch Creek and spooked Mr. Cuddy's camel. Mr. Cuddy was dumped on top of the iron door.

Squinting beyond Mt. Pinos, I could see Lake Buena Vista shimmering with blue water.

"Garrett."

Instinctively, the antique double-barreled shotgun fired. A shadow slipped off the fallen 28th Jeffrey.

"Dunham," I said, chocolate bars spilling from my shirt pocket.

"I'm good, Kay," he said. Blood from his hip spattered the bank of Butterscotch Creek.

"Sorry, Dun. Damn gun has a mind of its own."

He said, "Doesn't hurt anymore. Besides, it was the Seville, not the gun."

"Why were you sitting on the log? Aren't you in the game?"

"I'm not playing. No one is forced to play the game. Your grandfather Harry Kay didn't play."

"Are you still armed?"

"Sure." He pulled out the Colt's from our dream on Half Dome. "Don't need it, though." He tossed the Colt's over his shoulder and it slapped the surface of Butterscotch Creek.

"Holy shit, there's water."

"I was only waiting for you," he said.

"Me?"

"Yeah, you."

"Why me?"

"Because you're my trading partner. You never fail to bring me a couple of pills."

I cursed myself for leaving all the drugs in my writing desk. It was thoughtless and stupid. At no other time in my life had I experienced such regret. Dunham realized my predicament and shrugged.

He said, "Well, if you had a couple of pills you'd hand them over. It's all the same."

"Fucked up," I admitted. Then I remembered the Halloween pills in my L.L. Bean hiking boot. "Wait, Dun." My heart began to pound. I fingered the inside of my left boot and four codeine pills plopped in my hand. "Hopefully this makes up for Half Dome resembling the Empire State Building."

"Only good memories," Dunham said. Dipping into his pocket, he threw me a small manila envelope. He knelt by the creek and lapped water. Inside the envelope was a mound of crystal flakes. Leaning against the fallen 28th Jeffrey, I poked my bloodied nose into the envelope and snorted.

"J. shot my petrified rock," I explained, sniffling.

"Remember the red-head from Yosemite? What was her name?"

"Julie Christie."

"Right, Julie Christie. In my dream on Half Dome, Julie Christie showed up at Hughes Supermarket."

"How could she have known about the accident?"

"Larson called her. She was at your apartment in Sepulveda."

I said, "No, Julie Christie was working at Valley Hospital. I saw her."

"She's not a nurse, Kay, she's your girlfriend. We're still in Hughes Supermarket."

"If you don't play the game, what are you going to do?"

"Well, I…"

"Tell me, Dun. What are you going to do?"

"Move on," he said.

"What exactly does that mean?"

"I'm going to die."

"Quit kidding."

"I'm staying in the other field with Woody. I can't come back to the cabin and watch *Night Gallery* with Rod Serling."

"But how are you going to die?"

"In the accident at Hughes Supermarket."

"That is not going to happen."

"Don't play dumb, Kay. You understand."

"When will you die?"

He looked me in the eye. "Now, right now."

A shelf of chili beans crashed to the tile floor, knocking Dunham into Butterscotch Creek. I sucked in my breath. Tightening my grip on the shotgun, I plunged into the frigid water.

"Larson," I shouted. "Larson, come here."

I thrashed under the surface and lunged at Dunham, but the chili bean cans swarmed in my face. Bobbing for air, I saw that I was fifty feet downstream and gaining momentum.

My second mental note came to mind—Butterscotch Creek can outrun me. Riding Mr. Cuddy's shotgun, I was swept over the shoals.

"Hey, Loco Loco," the cop who shot himself said. I was groping in the dust of a dried creek bed and a black Lab was licking my face. "Might run faster if you used your legs."

I said, "How'd you make it to Lake of the Woods?"

"Used the password."

"What password?"

"Blue Mountain, of course."

"But how did you find me?"

"Him," he said, pointing to the Lab.

"WOODY!"

"He led me right to this dusty old creek bed." Butterscotch Creek was indeed bone dry.

I said, "Mr. Cuddy leaked the news of your recovery. Well played."

"I came to Lake of the Woods to help you."

"How?"

"After we stopped fucking with each other, I learned a few things."

"You helped me too."

"Listen to me, Kay. You're looking into a reflection in a freezer door."

"No way."

"Down there." He pointed. Rugged Iris Ridge jutted toward Maray Point and the great southern oak. "You must go in the opposite direction."

"But…"

"I'm serious. It's a trick."

"How can you be certain?"

"Trust me. You're looking into a reflection. Iris Ridge is in the opposite direction."

I said, "That sneaky bastard."

"No joke, Kay. Mr. Cuddy is no ordinary man."

"Okay, I'll do it."

"Good. Now you can recover."

"According to J., I'm in the lead."

The cop said, "Look, Kay, Woody forgives me for shooting him."

The Lab lifted his paw.

I said, "You've been a true friend. I won't forget you."

"We'll play Monopoly soon."

"With chardonnay, of course."

"But first you must win the game."

"Will you take Woody back to his field? Dunham is going to stay with him."

"Sure, Woody and me are big pals."

I looked at the big black Lab. "Don't be afraid anymore, Woody. I know you've been hiding."

At Hughes Supermarket, an ambulance siren wailed in the parking lot. When Larson wiped the hair out of his eyes, I noticed his hands were smeared with red, sticky blood.

I said, "I thought you were supposed to keep the blood inside my leg."

"Shut up, Kay. There's blood everywhere."

Dunham had been correct about Julie Christie. She knelt by my side and combed my hair with her hot and moist fingers. She said, "I'm going with you to the hospital."

Suddenly, it sounded like a tank had driven into Hughes Supermarket. Larson said, "What the fuck is that?"

"Run, Larson. It's Mr. Cuddy on his bulldozer."

"See you on the other side when this is finished."

"Other side of what?"

"Sierra del Ajo."

Cocaine burst into my bloodstream. Crackling with electricity, I broke into a mountain slipping frenzy. It was the L.A City Cross Country Finals of

1964. At the urging of Coach Godfrey, I had finally uncorked one. The great southern oak was less than four hundred yards down the Pierce College course.

On the nape of my neck was slobber. To my far right, Larson tried desperately to keep up, but my momentum was too strong. The cop who shot himself cheered wildly from his hospital bed. Mr. Cuddy was nowhere in sight.

As I approached Maray Point, the great southern oak stood directly in my path. Wherever I went on Blue Mountain, that tree seemed to follow. The image of Jack Palance on its trunk was unmistakable. I became hesitant and queasy. I sensed that a fiendish trap had been set in motion. As I gathered strength for my final leap off Iris Ridge, the great southern oak shed its bark and transformed into Mr. Cuddy.

"Nice trick," I yelled. It had been a brilliant disguise.

Mr. Cuddy raised his hand with the intention of blocking my charge. Lowering my head, like Crazy Legs Hirsh, I bowled him over and sailed off Maray Point.

With the crack of a single shot from Mr. Cuddy's Colt's, a dollop of blood spit out my nose. Nothing could prevent a crash landing. The accident at Hughes Supermarket hadn't laid a finger on Larson.

"I never lock the door of Cuddy Ski and Toboggan Rentals," Mr. Cuddy said, looking down at me.

"You mean I didn't have to climb that fucking fence?"

He grinned. "You're a wiseass, Garrett."

I said, "No matter, Mr. Cuddy. I won and you know it. You cheated."

"That's very true. I was licked fair and square. You've earned a reprieve."

I blew more blood out my nose. "May I borrow your bandana? My bleeding has gotten out of control."

"You're not hurt," he assured me. "It's only the game." He wiped my nose with his bandana and the blood was gone. "Very few have forced me to fire the weaponry. I use it only when I've been whipped. You gave a courageous performance." He bowed slightly and started to trudge back up Iris Ridge.

I said, "Mr. Cuddy?"

He stopped. "Final question, Kay."

"What's it like to know no more?"

He turned and looked me in the eye. With the malicious drawl of Jack Palance, he said, "There is no such thing."

FORTY-FOUR
Return to Hughes Supermarket

Star Trek

Like a mammoth starship, Hughes Supermarket settled on Maray Point.

Pressing a moist finger to Ms. D.'s throat, Julie Christie shook her head. Larson helped Henry the dog vet apply a tourniquet. In the parking lot, the ambulance siren had been turned off.

Larson said, "Medics are running up aisle nine."

"Don't let them forget J."

"You beat the old guy, didn't you?"

I nodded.

Acknowledgments

I want to thank Todd Carstenn, Bruce Balliet, Mary Ann Wilkinson, Laurie Werts and Elaine Springer Kent for their faith and support.

Thank you to Hal Zina Bennett at Tenacity Press for help and advice, and to R. V. Schmidt for *Abel Stover*.

Special thanks to my editor Daniel Barth for insight, guidance, *Fast Women Beautiful,* and the reminder about Groucho's $100 duck. This book was laboring on the hills until you saw that it had the legs and the heart to go the distance.

About the Author

G. Kent lives in the wilds of the Ocala National Forest in north Florida. He was born and raised in Los Angeles. *Bandits on the Rim* is his first novel. For more information contact kentib@earthlink.net.

Made in the USA
Lexington, KY
13 December 2012